I0632591

Thomas Hill

In the Woods and elsewhere

Thomas Hill

In the Woods and elsewhere

ISBN/EAN: 9783744642378

Printed in Europe, USA, Canada, Australia, Japan

Cover: Foto ©Andreas Hilbeck / pixelio.de

More available books at **www.hansebooks.com**

IN THE WOODS

AND ELSEWHERE

BY

THOMAS HILL

BOSTON

CUPPLES AND HURD

Publishers

1888

THIS SELECTION

FROM MY SCATTERED VERSES

IS AFFECTIONATELY DEDICATED TO

The Young Ladies' Sewing Circle of the First Parish,

WHOSE KIND RECEPTION OF A SMALLER SELECTION,

PRIVATELY PRINTED UNDER THE SAME

TITLE, LED TO THIS.

PREFACE.

THESE Verses are selected from a scrap-book which it has taken over forty years to fill. The larger part of them came to me unsought while I was driving my horse or resigning myself to the movement of the railway-train. Goethe somewhere says that such spontaneous verses are the truest revelation of the man who writes them.

PORTLAND, MAINE, 1888.

CONTENTS.

8 *Contents.*

Contents.

9

PAGE

TRANSLATIONS AND IMITATIONS.

IN THE WOODS.

" In the woods we return to reason and faith."

In the woods on an April day,
When the bluebirds whistle low,
    And song-sparrows trill
    Their quaint little ditty,
    Mid moss-covered trees,
    Over last year's leaves,
    I stroll; and my heart
    Leaps up and sings
    Like a bird in the early spring.
The little windflower peeps up to greet me,
Seeming to laugh in the April sun;
The hepatica opens its pale blue eye,
And trustingly looks at the deep blue heaven.

I look up too, — I cannot say why;
For the springs of hope and the tide of joy
Flow from the earth as from the sky:
Below, as above, one promise shines;
Below, as above, one Presence glows.

In the woods, in early June,
The oriole pipes so clear;
From meadows below
The bobolink pours
His frolicsome lay;
And over me sing
The catbird and thrush;
To whose jubilant notes
My heart keeps beating time.
The promise, now fulfilment grown,
The Presence in dear Summer glows;
Its beauty is more than heart can hold.
The leafy ocean overhead,
The flower-girt shore on which I stand,
Alike are infinite in forms
Of life, in beauty infinite.
In vain I strive to drink all in,
In vain to utter all I feel.

When under August suns
All Nature faints, I wander
    To the woods, and dream
    In the deep cool shade;
    While the vireo calls,
    And cicadas shrill,
    Mid the branches, tell
Of the heat I no longer feel.
From the woodland swamp a lazy breeze,
Stealing along with noiseless step,
Brings the white-robed clethra's breath,
And the velvet apios' grape-like odor.
Nor song of bird, nor sight of beauty,
Fills the heart with more calm delight.
Through every sense I draw in bliss;
Each sight, each sound, each odor tells
Of one all-loving Presence there.

    To the woods October calls
    My willing feet, to find
        Mid the golden-rod
        And the falling leaves
        Of the maple-trees,
        With their varied hues,

Or of scarlet oaks,
Or the crimson gum,
The crown of the beauteous year.
In the rich, ripe leaves of the autumn woods,
After the summer's pride is o'er,
A glory glows like a sunset sky.
All change is glorious : in the work
Of the world's Builder naught turns back;
Each change brings in new excellence.
The sunset of the year foretells,
To the trusting heart, a sunrise glad
In the woods, when the bluebirds come again.

And when January snows,
With a glittering robe of white,
Have hidden the fields,
The chickadee sings
His inspiriting song ;
And asks me to come
With him, to enjoy
In the quiet woods
The charm of a winter's day.
His cheery note, and the chickaree's chatter,
Rather reveal than break the silence.
The hemlock and pine, if the wind should call,

Scarce could, with snowflakes muffled, answer;
Nor yet the sun, with his soft persuasion,
Is luring the snow to leave the branches.
No sound prevents the full enjoyment
Of form and color, in the trees and rocks,
And purple shadows on the snow.

To the woods, to the woods I go,
Whate'er my frame of mind;
And find my heart
Is there attuned
To holy thought.
In woods I see,
And forests wild,
A husbandry rare;
And the husbandman is God.
In the presence there my soul awakes,
Each passion cools, while faith grows strong.
My little plans of life forgot,
I live, for the time, in the life of God.
With Him I tend each tree and plant,
Each creature feed, all Nature fill;
Then, strong in energy divine,
Back to my little sphere return;
Lo! He comes with me, — makes it His.

SYMPLOCARPUS.

Mid alder bushes by the stream
I stroll, of coming Spring to dream,
While yet the drifts of Winter's snow
Seem loath from shaded spots to go,
And e'en the sun can scarce induce
The frost, by day, to grant a truce.

The alder catkins safe enfold,
As yet, their pollen from the cold ;
Nor any flower has dared to bring
The promise of returning Spring.

Nay ! say not so, but pause and look !
Those islands in the sluggish brook
Have each a little coronet,
With garnets and with emeralds set.
Within those hoods, of royal hue,
There lies, concealed from careless view,

In each a globe of flowers ; the first
From Winter's loosening chains to burst.

Thrice welcome! earliest flower of Spring!
Thy praise, but not thy name, I sing.
Ungrateful men have christened thee
With names unkind, unsavory.
Because when they, with wanton tread,
Their crushing heel set on thy head,
Thou dost resent so foul a wrong,
They give thee names unfit for song.
Vain is their spite, while thus my verse
Thy praise and merit shall rehearse.
And oft as woodland memories bring
The pleasant thoughts of early Spring,
Welcome, among them all, to me
Thy face without a name shall be.

THE MARSH.

HERE, under the moss, even in midsummer,
Cool water is found, oozing out silently;
Soon filling the prints left by my footsteps, while
I, sauntering on, seek for my favorites, —
Flowers such as the marsh only can give to me.

This marsh might be thought wasted in idleness:
No husbandman finds profit in tilling it;
Ne'er fragrant with hay, merry with haymakers;
Ne'er golden with grain, snowy with buckwheat, nor
E'er covered with maize, stately and beautiful.
Yet boldly I say: Never an acre of
Rich arable land yields, to my gathering,
Fruits richer than those ever awaiting me
When hither I come gathering wild-flowers.
Here, spicy and sweet, breathes Arethusa in
May, — beautiful nymph, robed in magnificence!
Here, also in May, blooms Menyanthes, the

Buckbean, with its soft delicate clusters of
Fringed lilac; in June, fragrant Pogonia
Half hides in the grass; while Sarracenia
Waves, over her cups, banners of purple; and
Sundew, at her feet, glitters with diamonds.
Then comes, in July, rich Calopogon, and
Gay Orchises glow; while the Gerardia
Buds, promising rare beauties in August; when
Sweet odors shall rise, breathed by Neottia.

Cease! Vain is the task. Who can enumerate,
Much less can describe, half of my favorites?
One more let me name: dearest of all is the
Fringed Gentian, which lifts, e'en in November, her
Bright face to the sun; teaching us constancy,
Faith, patience to bear frosts of adversity;
Sweet lessons of love, God's gentle messages.
What fruits of a field tilled by the husbandman
Yield better returns, blessings more actual?

TO A PRAIRIE ROSE.

ON HEARING A COMPLAINT THAT IT IS SCENTLESS.

ALL things are not to each thing given,
Then why seek all from thee, bright Rose?
Enough for me thy clustering flowers;
Thy gay and glorious garlands fill
With joy and gladness all my thankful heart;
And full as quickly would I ask for fruit,
As ask for odor, from thy flowery wreath.

As through my door I look on yonder grove
Of oaks majestic, bathed in noontide light, —
Their branches heaving like a boiling sea
Of foliage, forest ocean of July, —
Is not their beauty perfect? Not thy wreaths
Could add, gay Rose, a tittle to their grace.

Each plant is perfect, each in its own way;
The mignonette asks not the tulip's show:

The phlox, no odor from the violet.
The very weeds are each one perfect flowers :
The knotgrass, with its emerald and pearl ;
The sandwort, offering noon its rosy cup ;
The northern toadflax, in a bonnet blue ;
The southern shining in a helm of gold ; —
Such plants as these, along the wayside found,
Are perfect flowers (weeds but when out of place),
And need of beauty nothing more to seek.
Much less, my Rose, needst thou for odor ask.

So must we be content to find, fair Rose,
Each man adapted to his proper sphere :
Perfect, if working after God's intent.
Oh, happy flowers, to know no will but His !
Far happier he who makes that will his own ;
Filling his station with unconscious ease ;
Giving like thee, dear Rose, to passers-by,
All undesigned, his gifts of worth untold ;
And, unlike thee, himself heart-full of bliss.

THE BALTIMORE ORIOLE.

Oh, golden robin! pipe again
That happy, hopeful, cheering strain!

A prisoner in my chamber, I
See neither grass, nor bough, nor sky;
Yet to my mind thy warblings bring,
In troops, all images of Spring;
And every sense is satisfied
By what thy magic has supplied.
As by enchantment, now I see,
On every bush and forest-tree,
The tender, downy leaf appear, —
The loveliest robe they ever wear.

The tulip and the hyacinth grace
The garden bed; each grassy place,
With dandelions glowing bright,
Or king-cups, childhood's pure delight,

Invite the passer-by to tread
Upon the soft elastic bed,
And pluck again the simple flowers
Which charmed so oft his younger hours.
The apple orchards all in bloom, —
I seem to smell their rare perfume.
And thou, gay whistler! to whose song
These powers of magic art belong,
On top of lofty elm I see
Thy black and orange livery —
Forgive that word! A freeman bold,
Of choice thou wearest jet and gold,
And no man's livery dost bear,
Thou flying tulip! free as air!

Come, golden robin! once again
That magic, joy-inspiring strain!

THE MILE RUN.

MILE RUN! Strange though it seem, nothing more
    musical
I hear uttered in speech, than the two syllables
Mile Run, — dear to my heart even from infancy.
Long years, burdened with care, buoyant with hap-
    piness,
Ne'er hid, never can hide, pictures that memory
Still draws from the Mile Run's beautiful scenery.

Here Spring's balmiest breath wakened the wild-
    flowers.
First came, after the snow, early hepaticas,
Pale blue, shrinking from sight ; then the claytonia,
Bright Spring Beauty ; and red honey-horned col-
    umbines ;
Soon sprang, tender and frail, quaint little breeches-
    plant ;
With these, fairest of all, rue-leaved anemones.

Hill-sides bordering the brook glowed with the
    beautiful
May phlox; while at the foot, under the alders,
    grew
Dog-tooth violets, called otherwise adder's tongue.

Here, when summer had come, gayly the clematis
Flung, o'er thickets of green, snowy-white drapery.
Then wild senna in bloom glowed through the
    underwood.
Then, too, dazzling red, glittered the cardinal.
Plum-trees, loaded with fruit, crimson and savory;
Mandrakes, juicy and sweet; luscious wild straw-
    berries;
Shellbarks, filberts, and sweet cloying persimmons,
    the
Mile Run yielded in days pictured by memory.

Scarce flows water where once barefoot I waded,
    and
No more blossom, as then, senna and clematis;
No more fringes the brook, plum-tree or bladdernut;
Yet still blooms in my heart each of the flowers
    that
E'er in childhood I saw bloom by that watercourse.

RUE–LEAVED ANEMONE.

Unconscious little innocent!
The only charm that is not lent
To thee, by Nature, is the grace
Of blushing at my earnest praise.

The sun more fondly smiles to see
This wooded knoll, because of thee;
These trees refrain a shade to cast
Until thy time of bloom be past;
And birds renew their tuneful mirth,
To see thee bursting from the earth!

At first thy little head peeps out
With purple leaves well wrapped about;
Fearing lest April suns may be
Still constant in inconstancy,
And lest late snow, or wintry rains,
May chill the blood within thy veins.

Then taking courage day by day,
As April still gives place to May,
The wrappers thou dost all unfold,
No longer purple with the cold,
And show thy beauty to the sky,
The joy of every passer-by.

Thy petals, delicate and fair,
The gentle grace that marks thine air,
Thy leaf so neat, and stem so frail, —
Thy charms uncounted cannot fail,
All unobtrusive as thou art,
To catch the eye and win the heart.
Yet let me not presumptuous be,
Or think it possible for me
To tell the reason that my flower
Has, over human hearts, such power.
No outward eye can beauty see ;
An inward sense alone can be
Percipient of its heavenly glow.
Nor can the understanding know
The secret causes that impart
The sense of beauty to the heart.

Rue-leaved Anemone! who knows
Why thou art dearer than the rose
To me, and why no other flower
Can move my heart with half thy power?
Perchance a subtle law may bind
Some idiosyncrasy of mind
In me with thy peculiar form.
Perchance it may my bosom warm
Toward thee, because in thee I trace
Some likeness to the human face;
And thou within my heart may share
The place of child or woman fair.

Perchance the secret lies too deep
For conscious scrutiny ; where sleep
A thousand long-forgotten hours,
Beyond our recollection's powers;
Yet tingeing, with their joys or woes,
The feelings current, as it flows;
And he who would the secret tell,
Why I should love this flower so well,
Those hidden memories must find,
Which secretly its beauties bind

To those who long since, through the tomb,
Sought flowers of amaranthine bloom.

Oh, hallowed Power within me ! still
My heart with thoughts of loved ones fill ;
And let each flower of coming Spring
A charm around their memory fling ;
My childhood's innocence restore,
Its faith and hope, forevermore.

NEW ENGLAND THRUSHES.

SLOWLY, in the hazy west,
Sinks the languid sun to rest;
Weary with his toil all day
On the steep ecliptic way.
Nearly has he reached his goal,
Bearing Summer toward the pole;
Short the path that now remains,
Ere the tropic he attains:
'T is the setting sun of May;
To-morrow June shall fill the day.

As the ruddy orb descends,
The gentle south wind sweetly blends
All the happy sounds of Spring:
Song of birds upon the wing,
Trill of toad and cry of frog, —
Ruder music of the bog
Mingled with the sweeter strains
From the woodlands and the plains.

But when light begins to fade,
Presaging a deeper shade,
All the birds except the thrushes
The departing sunlight hushes.
Bobolink no more, so gay,
Swings and rattles on the spray;
Nor the oriole's piping clear
Rings upon the listening ear;
Chattering sparrows all have ceased,
And the vireo is released
From his self-imposèd task
To tell his name though no one ask.

But this holy hour of rest
Fills with joy the thrush's breast;
All the family unite
In welcome to the coming night.
From the time that bobolink ceases
His exultant, merry strain,
Till the whippoorwill shall sadly
To the moon and stars complain,
All the thrushes join in chorus,
As the shades of night come o'er us,
Singing evening hymns of praise

In melodious, varied lays.
The wandering thrush with cheerful tone
(As the robin better known),
The catbird with a liquid song,
And Wilson's thrush with trumpet tongue,
The wood-thrush singing wild and free,
The brown thrush chanting joyously, —
These all swell the sacred chorus,
As the twilight deepens o'er us.

Happy thrushes! if your faith,
Piercing through the gloom of night,
Seeing more than others see,
See the morrow's coming light!
When the evening sun of life
Sheds its mellow beams on me,
May my thoughts, my hope, and faith,
Like the song of thrushes be!
Naught but praise employ my breath
As I meet the night of death,
Looking, without fear or sorrow,
For the resurrection's morrow!

THE AMERICAN ROBIN.

THE sun is set, the west is bright;
    The robin, on the apple-bough,
Without a fear of coming night,
    Still sings, " The happiest hour is now."

The piping frog calls out, "Good-night!"
    And jewelled toads prolong their trill;
To them the darkness is as light,
    While May-day pulses through them thrill.

Soft o'er the highlands and the vale
    The south wind breathes its promises,
That summer's harvest shall not fail,
    And autumn fruit shall bend the trees.

O gladness, heightened yet with hope,
    Looking through darkness into light,
Through midnight seeing morning ope,
    With coming May November bright,

Still fill my heart, nor suffer fear
  And doubt to close my faithless sight
Against the morning that appears
  All glowing with eternal light!

THE BOBOLINK.

BOBOLINK! that in the meadow
Or beneath the orchard's shadow
Keepest up a constant rattle,
Joyous as my children's prattle;
Welcome to the North again!
Welcome to mine ear thy strain;
Welcome to mine eye the sight
Of thy black, thy buff, and white.
Brighter plumes may greet the sun
By the banks of Amazon;
Sweeter tones may weave the spell
Of enchanting Philomel;
But the tropic bird would fail,
And the English nightingale,
If we should compare their worth
With thine endless gushing mirth.

When the Ides of May are past,
June and Summer nearing fast,

While from depths of blue above
Comes the mighty breath of love,
Calling out each bud and flower
With resistless, secret power ;
Waking hope and fond desire ;
Kindling the erotic fire ;
Filling youths' and maidens' dreams
With mysterious, pleasing themes, —
Then, amid the sunlight clear,
Floating in the fragrant air,
Thou dost fill each heart with pleasure
By thy glad, ecstatic measure.

A single note, so sweet and low,
Like a full heart's overflow,
Forms the prelude ; but the strain
Gives us no such tone again.
For the wild and saucy song
Leaps and skips the notes among,
In such quick and sportive play,
Ne'er was madder, merrier lay.

Gayest songster of the Spring !
Thy melodies before me bring

Visions of some dream-built land,
Where, by constant zephyrs fanned,
I might walk the livelong day,
Embosomed in perpetual May.
Nor care nor fear thy bosom knows;
For thee a tempest never blows;
But, when our Northern Summer's o'er,
By Delaware or Schuylkill's shore,
The wild-rice lifts its airy head,
And royal feasts for thee are spread.
Then, when the winter threatens there,
Thy tireless wings yet own no fear,
But bear thee to more southern coasts,
Far beyond the reach of frosts.

Bobolink! still may thy gladness
Drive from me all taint of sadness;
Fill my soul with trust unshaken
In that Being who has taken
Care for every living thing,
In summer, winter, fall, and spring!

.

SUNRISE AND SUNSET.

HE who will rise and watch the morning rise,
Will, as he gazes, find his bosom swell
With gratitude too deep for words toward Him
Who taught the dayspring thus to know its place,
And formed the eye its loveliness to see!
So he who notes the softened evening glow
Shall find his heart uplifted by the sight
In silent prayer, to be admitted where
Nor night nor morning comes, but ever there
The evening time is light with endless day.

THE EARLIEST FIRE–FLY.

FEARLESS little pioneer,
Leader of thy race this year !
Tiny spark of wondrous light,
Wandering thro' the darksome night
Strangely pleasant is the sight
Of thy vague, erratic flight.

Soon thy light will be but lost,
Mid thy fellows' brilliant host,
When the meadow lands shall be
Gay with mimic galaxy.

Finches prophesy the Spring,
Bobolinks its blossoms bring ;
But thy race, with bolder cheer,
Say that Summer now is here.
Now the wild grape fills the air
With a wealth of perfume rare ;

Roses bloom beside the way,
Joy and fragrance fill the day;
Now the sunlight's lengthened hours
Ring with song and glow with flowers.
Leader of the glittering band
Soon to follow thy command,
Welcome, then, thou tiny spark,
Seen against the woodland dark!

Who had taught thee, underground,
Ere thy wings thou yet hadst found,
Who had taught thee thus to soar,
Thus to flit the meadows o'er,
Ere as yet thy cheering flame
From its hiding-places came?

Never yet another's light
Having met thy new-born sight,
How wilt thou the difference know
'Twixt a mate's and rival's glow?
How distinguish, in the dark,
Either from a glow-worm's spark?
Wonderful the mystery —
What shall safely pilot thee,

With unerring thread of fate
To thine only rightful mate?

Wanderer! thus unto my sight
With more than stellar lustre bright!
Ah! how gladly would I share
Courage which can boldly dare
Thus to mount on untried wing;
Boldly thus thyself to fling,
Whither heart within thee leads,
Toward higher life and nobler deeds!

Thus thou op'nest to mine eye
Scenes above this star-paved sky.
He who guides thy feeble race,
Pours on man a richer grace.

Outward eye hath never seen
Canaan's fields of living green;
Outward senses hear no song
Sung the eternal choirs among;
But the Son of God inspires,
In his saints, those warm desires,

And that strong, unconquered will
Which the heart with rapture fill.
When he calls, they soar away,
Freed from all this mortal clay,
Finding true the joyous word:
" Still together with the Lord."

A SMOKY DAY.

AND this is Burnell Hill, of local fame!
Here, when the air is clear, the eye can sweep
From Ossipee to Kennebec; from sea
To highest summit of the mountain chain
Between the Atlantic and the mighty stream
Fed by Niagara's changeless flood. To-day
Naught is in sight beyond the nearest range
Of neighboring hills. Southward, Sebago holds
In vain its lovely mirror to the sky;
In vain the northern hills point up toward heaven.
But most I miss the western majesty;
Hidden, Chocorua's bold and rugged form,
Pequawket's cone, the vast and varied mass
Of Agiochook; all hid in murky night
At midday. E'en these lower hills, which spring
Out of the nearest valley, have an air
Of unsubstantialness; they seem but smoke.

The vision which we climbed to see is hid;
But better visions, to the inward eye,

May teach the lesson of this smoky day.
This hazy air harms not the thing it hides;
The Saco and Presumpscot seaward flow,
Pequawket skyward points, the same to-day
As when northwesters blow away the mist
So clean that furthest distance is not blue;
Yon coppery globe, — 't is still the blessed sun,
Resplendent in his sphere.

                    Thus, doubting soul,
Thus harmless are the mists which error breeds,
And wide delusions spread; they hurt no truth.
A truth, once seen in vision clear, is true,
Though every eye grew dim, and blear with smoke,
Enfolding nations in a dark eclipse.
The eternal sun still shines behind the cloud,
And cool Siloam's shady rill still flows;
The threatening heights of Horeb are unmoved;
From Zion still proceeds the eternal law;
The mount of the beatitudes endures;
The hill where Peter longed to stay; the mount
Where the great sufferer hung upon the cross;
And Olivet from which he rose to heaven.
The smoke which hides the temporal world from sight
Does not destroy it; nor does error's cloud
Do aught to harm eternal verities.

A SUMMER EVENING.

THE crescent moon is sinking,
 The star-lit hours are nigh;
From yonder wood comes floating
 The whippoorwill's lone cry;
And there the wild grape blooming
 Perfumes the gentle breeze;
While fire-flies weave their mazes,
 And flicker mid the trees.

THE HYMN OF NIAGARA.

HERE stand! here, from the flood raving unceas-
    ingly,
Hoarse shrill murmurs arise; shrill as the wind,
    when it
      Roars thro' the trees stripped of their foliage,
      Singing its wild anthem of liberty.

With these come to the ear, ever at intervals,
Quick notes, rattling and sharp; like the artillery
      Heard when a storm, driving up rapidly,
      Crashes the oaks down with its thunderbolts.

Now rise, muffled in mist, rolling up heavily,
Deep tones, awfully grand, shaking the earth, as
    they
      Swell like the low bass of the thunderstorm,
      Heard by the strained ear of the listener.

Thus float over the mist, ever in harmony,
Three tones, joyous and free, forming Niagara's
    Anthem of praise, new every moment, yet
    Changeless as time, old as eternity.

THE MOUNTAINS.

THE mountains in winter, the mountains I love :
Below, the black forest; the white peaks, above;
Along the calm valleys, the deep drifted snow ;
While over the summits the winter winds blow ;
The moose and the deer through the underwood
        roam,
And the chickadee finds in the fir-trees a home.

The mountains in spring-time, the mountains I love;
When soft through the valleys the warm breezes
        move ;
While swift-rushing torrents are bearing away
The ice, which so long in their recesses lay ;
The little wild-flowers fear no longer the cold,
And the birch and the poplar their catkins unfold.

The mountains in summer, the mountains I love :
Below, the green birches; the gray peaks above ;

Along the calm valleys the crystal brooks flow ;
The flowers on the summits are white as the snow ;
The deep forests ring, at the close of the day,
With the white-throated Peverley's sweet roundelay.

The mountains in autumn, the mountains I love ;
All clothed in full glories, below and above :
In purple and gold, scarlet, crimson, and brown, —
Royal garments below ; and above, a white crown.
Oh ! the beauty and richness of all the long year
Are reserved for the hills in October to wear.

———•———

FROM THE GREEK.

I ASK not for pleasures ; I ask not for wealth ;
But give me contentment, and give me good health.

THE BLACK-CAP TITMOUSE.

WHEN the purple morning glow
Crimsons the new-fallen snow,
Then the tomtit whistles free,
Cheerily singing "Chickadee?"

What recks he of winter storm?
Fir and cedar keep him warm;
Moss-grown branches at his side
Show a larder well supplied.

North winds howl o'er hill and plain,
Frost-stars deck the window-pane;
He, from out the thick fir-tree,
Greets the day with "Chickadee!"

THE WINTER IS PAST.

Soft, on this April morning,
Breathe, from the south, delicate odors
Vaguely defined, giving the breezes
Springlike, delicious zest; —

Breezes from southern forests,
Bringing us glad tidings of Summer's
Promised return ; waking from slumber
Each of the earliest plants.

Lo ! in the night, the elm-tree
Opened its buds; catkins of hazel
Tasselled the hedge ; maple and alder
Welcomed with bloom the Spring.

Faintly the warbling bluebird
Utters his note ; song-sparrows boldly
Fling to the wind joyous assurance
" Summer is coming north."

None can express the longing,
Mingled with joy, mingled with sadness,
Swelling my heart ever, when April
Brings us the bird and flower.

Tender and sweet remembrance,
Filling my soul, gives me assurance :
" Death is but frost. Lo ! the eternal
Springtime of heaven shall come."

CARPE DIEM.

BUILD not on to-morrow,
  But seize on to-day!
From no future borrow,
  The present to pay.

Wait not any longer
  Thy work to begin;
By work we grow stronger;
  Be steadfast and win.

Forebode not new sorrow;
  Bear that of to-day,
And trust that to-morrow
  Shall chase it away.

The task of the present
  Be sure to fulfil;
If irksome, or pleasant,
  Be true to it still.

God sendeth us sorrow,
    And cloudeth our day;
His sun on the morrow
    Shines bright on our way.

BLOODROOT.

" Loved the wild rose, and left it on its stalk ? "

BEECH-TREES, stretching their arms, rugged yet
    beautiful,
Here shade meadow and brook; here the gay
    bobolink,
High poised over his mate, pours out his melody.
Here too, under the hill, blooms the wild violet ;
Damp nooks hide, near the brook, bellworts that
    modestly,
Pale-faced, hanging their heads, droop there in
    silence, while
South winds, noiseless and soft, bring us the odor of
Birch twigs mingled with fresh buds of the hickory.

Hard by, clinging to rocks, nods the red columbine ;
Close-hid, under the leaves, nestle anemones,
White-robed, airy and frail, tender and delicate.

Ye who, wandering here, seeking the beautiful,
Stoop down, thinking to pluck one of these
    favorites,
Take heed! nymphs may avenge. List to a prodigy!
One moon scarcely has waned since I here wit-
    nessed it.
One moon scarcely has waned since, on a holiday,
I came, careless and gay, into this paradise;
Found here, wrapped in their cloaks made of a leaf,
    little
White flowers, pure as the snow, modest and in-
    nocent;
Stooped down, eagerly plucked one of the fairest;
    when
Forth rushed, fresh from the stem broken thus
    wickedly,
Blood! — tears, red as of blood, — shed through
    my selfishness.

AGNES' STAR.

EARLY in June I wandered in the woods,
Ere last year's leaves were dry. The ground was
    strewn
With delicate and seven-pointed stars,
White as six-pointed stars which fall from heaven,
And, like them, half transparent. Though I stooped,
To gain a nearer view, I did not seek,
Sempronius-like, to pluck the flower ; nor gave
Some future Tintoretto's pencil scope.
But as I bowed and silent gazed, I thought
That when the Swedish Adam named the plants,
His wonted inspiration failed him here ;
And, with Linnæus' leave, I 'd henceforth call
Our northern Trientalis, — Agnes' Star.

HYMN OF THE SEASONS.

THE early violets, springing from the sod;
The saxifrage that blooms beside the rock;
The softly swelling lawn, besprinkled o'er
With falling flowers of maple and of elm,
And watered by the gently flowing brook,
Beside whose edge the golden caltha lifts
Its cheerful face; anemones, bloodroot,
And adder's tongue;—the wild-flowers, each and all,
With one accord, reveal one boundless love;
They show to man the glorious name of God.

The hum of early-waking bees; the note
Of sparrows, gossiping with merry tongue;
The cheerful sunset song of thrush, misnamed,
Yet honoring the robin's name he bears;
The piping frog's good-night; the toad's long trill;—
These all blend sweetly in the chord of hope,
That fills the soul with longing and with tears,

Awaking thoughts of childhood; spring-time
    sweet
Of life, — when God dwelt in an unstained heart.

In June, on yonder wooded hill, go sit
Beneath the leafy trees ; where, overhead,
The brown thrush, playful, taunts the farmer's toil ;
The catbird sings his ever-varied lay ;
While from the elm, amid the neighboring mead,
The oriole his clear bold whistle sounds ;
And, from the mead itself, the bobolink pours
His liquid prelude and his saucy song.
In all this flood of melody one sound
Will ever fill thine ear, — the name of God.

Around thy seat the flowers of June will rise,
To fill thine eye, with tokens of the Hand
That formed these merry songsters of the air.
The winter-loving herb pipsissewa
Adorns the Summer with a flower so neat,
That the most careless eye is caught and charmed.
The cranesbill lifts its slight and graceful head,
And the blue lupine makes the sandhill gay.
Go to the meadow ; gather there, with care,

The frailest and the loveliest of the flowers,
The orchis tribe; — the Arethusa, rich
In purple half transparent, and a breath
As richly spicy as the myrtle leaf;
Or the pogonia, modestly concealed,
With hanging head, amid the blue-eyed grass,
Spreading a perfume fitting to its grace;
Or calopogon, boastful of its wealth
Of purple beauty, holding perfume cheap.

Nor is the hand of the great Architect
Concealed, when ripening forest leaves display
The glories of October; joyous, yet
With chastened gladness seeming to recall,
Amid the glorious present, saddened thoughts
Of Summer past, and Winter drawing nigh.
Sad not to all; for they whose task is done,
And they who still toil on, with manful hearts,
To do the Father's will, drink in the flood
Of beauty from October scenery,
Without the draught of bitter memories.
How glows anew the Summer, in the leaf
Of hickory and birch; beforehand glow
The fires of Winter in the scarlet oak

And crimson tupelo. The maple bough
Bedecks itself with every brilliant hue.
Beside it, in a hyacinthine dress
Of sombre beauty, stands the rich-robed ash.
No tree, no plant, but now assumes a hue
In harmony with the autumnal scene.
The bramble that we scorned in June, we now
Can look on only with admiring eyes;
The very sorrel, that we warred against,
Is now a picture which delights our soul.

And when the leafy honors of the wood
Have fallen 'neath the approaching Winter's breath,
Come to the meads again, to gather now
The blue-fringed gentian, flower of hope and faith.
While every flower declares our Maker's love,
And lights with hope our life's quick changing year,
This above all; which, mid the piercing frosts,
And under bleak November's dreary sky,
Lifts thus its matchless azure, to revive   .
Our torpid faith, and cheer desponding hearts.

Yet why should Winter thus be feared by man?
For He who feeds the merry chickadee,

And guards the squirrel's safely hoarded store,
Keeps man beneath his ever-watchful eye;
He shows his children, mid the wintry storm,
The tokens of his presence and his love.
When the northeaster howls along our coast,
And blinding snowflakes fill the thickened air:
While short-lived day gives place to tedious night,
And double darkness clothes the earth and sky,
We lift a prayer for sea-tossed mariners,
But a new gush of gratitude wells up
For all the comforts of New England home.
Returning day, at length, unveils the scene:
The storm is hushed; the gently falling flakes,
Descending from a thin dissolving cloud,
Are clothing tree and shrub in whitest garb.
The sun breaks forth; the dazzled eye, in vain,
Attempts to gaze upon the glorious earth,
Too beautiful, too fair, for mortal sight.

Thus, in each season of the changing year,
Unchanging Love displays its boundless wealth;
In varied beauty, full-toned harmony,
And works of power and wisdom infinite.

ART AND NATURE.

THE artist calls the marble into life,
Or spreads the glowing landscape from his brush,
Not to enlarge the boundaries of sense,
But to convey a thought, or touch the heart.

Nor have the woods and fields, the lakes and brooks,
A lowlier purpose in creation's plan.
If man's rude imitations have such power,
Much more the originals, — the work of God.
Through each event, each season, and 'each thing
He breathes an all-persuasive eloquence,
Winning the hearts of men, and giving each
A share in wisdom's rich inheritance.

Through every part of Nature, great or small,
God's attributes of wisdom, power, and love
Are leading still his children to advance
In knowledge, diligence, and charity.

In every tone of Nature, — when, in Spring,
The gentle south wind, bathing every sense
In a delicious transport, brings each sound
With unaccustomed clearness to the ear, —
Or in the varied song of birds, when June
Makes all the beauty of the Spring forgot, —
Or when, in August, deep-dyed clouds
Announce the rising gust, and thunders deep
Wake all the solemn harmonies of heaven;
In every tone of Nature, — thundered, sighed,
Or flowing in a stream of melody, — one voice
Is ever uttered: 't is the voice of God.

In every field the glory of the Lord
Appears; to eyes devout, as visible
As once on Judah's plains, when in the night
The darkness melted, 'neath the herald dawn
Which to the shepherd swains foretold the rise
Of David's Son, the Sun of Righteousness.

Why, then, shall Allston's magic light and shade,
Or why Beethoven's chords, with deeper power,
Awake a holier glow within my heart,
Than that which springs from every daily sight

And every daily sound? For every sight
Is truly picture, drawn with infinite skill,
Shaded and colored with a matchless grace;
And every sound is music to the ear
That finds its sure relation to the key
Of Nature's universal harmony.

5

TO A PHYSALIA.

THE PORTUGUESE MAN-OF-WAR.

·   WHITHER, on pathless seas,
And tossed by restless billows to and fro,
Thy sails all spread to catch the favoring breeze,
        Say, whither dost thou go?

        Not like the wandering bird,
With sight of distant coast, or island near,
Or sound familiar, from below far heard,
        To aid his course to steer, —

        Not thus thou sailest by:
Thou passest boldly out of sight of land;
The trackless wave below; above, the sky, —
        No guide on either hand.

Peaceful republic! tell
What counsels guide thee on thy prosperous way;
What magic force thy members can compel,
    Wise counsels to obey.

Each seeks the public good;
Each labors, not for self but for the State;
Each does the part by him best understood,
    The part assigned by fate.

Nay, not by fate! The Power
Which guides so well what first it did create,
And gifted thee with wisdom's heavenly dower,
    Is holier than fate.

Power that dost guide aright,
Through air and sea, the creatures thou hast made,
Our hope for human states is on thy might,
    Thy loving wisdom, stayed.

A NOVEMBER PROBLEM.

WHILE the cars roll smoothly on, I gaze
　Toward the glowing evening sky;
Does form or color charm me most,
　In the landscape flitting by?

The marshes stretch their grassy sea
　Mid wooded isle and shore;
And swelling knoll and hill repeat
　The landscape o'er and o'er.

Each forest pine and fir tree points
　Its finger still on high;
The white birch delicately spreads
　Its twigs against the sky.

The triple bar of narrow clouds,
　Low arching all the west,
Seems motionless as leaf and tree;
　All Nature stands at rest.

Between those ruddy golden bars,
  How soft the emerald hue!
What harmony of glowing tints
  Leads upward to the blue!

The marshes and the fields are clothed
  In quiet robes of gray;
But rich the rosy purple blush
  Upon the birchen spray.

How thrilling was that sudden flash
  Of crimson light, which broke,
As the golden radiance through it streamed,
  From a passing grove of oak!

While thus clouds, woods, and fields sweep on
  Before my moistened eye,
Does form or color move me most,
  In the landscape hurrying by?

The eternal thought in form is seen,
  The eternal love in color glows;
Love prompts the thought, thought guides the love,
  And thus from both one influence flows.

ANTIOPA.

At dead of night a southwest breeze
  Came silently stealing along;
The bluebird followed, at break cf day,
  Singing his low, sweet song.

The breeze crept through the old stone wall;
  It wakened the butterfly there;
And she came out, as morning broke,
  To float through the sunlit air.

Within this stony, rifted heart
  The softening influence stole,
Filling with melodies divine
  The chambers of my soul;

With gentle words of hope and faith,
  By lips now sainted spoken;
With vows of tenderest love toward me,
  Which never once were broken.

At morn my soul awoke to life,
   And glowed with faith anew.
The buds that perish swelled without;
   Within, the immortal grew.

QUANDO VENIET LUX?

In this green lane we often walked,
  And oft my heart within me burned,
  As did the hearts of those returned
From Emmaus, who with Christ had talked.

The golden hand of Spring has thrown
  Again the king-cup by the hedge,
  And strewed with calthas yonder sedge;
But I walk down the lane alone.

No Spring's returning hand has power
  To bring thee to my side again;
  The south wind woos the grave in vain;
In vain the sun, or vernal shower.

The bobolink soars, as soars the lark,
  And pours his sweetness o'er the lawn;
  Rejoicing in the earliest dawn
The more, the more the night was dark.

A deeper darkness death, than night;
  When shall its awful shadows break?
  Its slumberers to life awake?
What songs shall hail that holier light?

FEBRUARY.

Oh, charmèd days! foretelling Spring
Before the earliest bluebirds sing.
What music from the tiny rills
Mid thawing snow on sunny hills!
What soothing softness in the air!
From swelling buds, what fragrance rare!
See, down the valley, how the haze
Is changing, even while we gaze,
Bare trees and rocks, with softened light,
To forms of beauty infinite.
Each mere suggestion of a thought
Is by the eager fancy caught,
And into summer scenery wrought.

This dreamy pleasure of the Spring,
Which hazy suns thus early bring,
Who shall define? Who tell, what part
Of all that fills and swells the heart,

Is from the actual present joy?
How much from fancy's fond employ?
The promised summer lends the spring
More joy than its own zephyrs bring.

Oh, type of all our human bliss!
The greater part still future is.
However bright the present days,
We ever turn our wistful gaze
Upon the future's mystic haze.
And I, herein, God's promise find
Written within the human mind,
That, while eternity shall roll,
Increasing joy shall fill the soul.

BIRDS IN MAY.

WHEN the sun early begins morn to awaken,
And his rays, piercing the gloom, scatter the dark-
    ness ;
While the flowers, children of May, silently open
All their sweets, making the air rich with their
    fragrance ;
And the birds, waking from sleep, warble their
    matins, —
I arise, throw up the sash, drink in their music,
Till my heart swells with a glad feeling of sympathy.

Merry notes ring through the copse, float o'er the
    meadow ;
Sounds of wild jubilant joy rise to my window ;
Yet the lark, plaintive and sad, joins in the chorus.

As I sit, watching the east glow in the dawning ;
As I muse, wrapped in the soft arms of the zephyr ;

As I thus, charmed by the birds, silently listen,
Swift the sun raises his brow o'er the horizon.

Then my ear catches a sound, borne from the
 chamber
Where reposed my little birds, —two of my children,
Whom the sun, throwing his rays in at their window,
Has aroused, rested by sleep, joyous and prattling.
Ah! what birds warble a song half so enchanting?

SUNRISE.

THE bobolink! again I hear,
The merriest bird of all the year.
As through my open window floats
The gladsome music of his notes,
Mingling with thrush and sparrow's song,
And tuneful rivals still prolong
The happy chorus, from my heart
The lingering shadows all depart.

The night was dark; and o'er my so
A thousand sad forebodings stole,
While memory's faithful glass had shown
As many joys forever flown.
I courted sleep, but yet my grief
Had found in slumber no relief;
For dreams and fearful visions still
Thronged in, my misery's cup to fill.

At length the daybreak, in the east,
My heart from fear in part released.
The small fly-catcher first awakes,
The second part the robin takes;
And then the wren and vireo
Begin with song to overflow.
The hangbird's clear and mellow tune,
And catbird's matins follow soon.
While richer grows the harmony,
Still from my soul the shadows flee.
But when, at last, from bobolink's throat
Bursts out the long-imprisoned note,
In liquid sweetness without measure,
Bubbling his ecstatic pleasure,
Then 't is sunrise in my heart.
In his pure joy I take a part;
And while he sings, I silent raise
My morning hymn of thanks and praise.

THE TEMPEST.

ALL night long the rain was falling;
  Torrents from the sky were poured;
Billows unto billows calling,
  Loud the sullen tempest roared.

Darkness brooded o'er the ocean,
  Earth and sky alike were black;
Felt and heard, not seen, the motion
  Threatening Nature's final wrack.

But at length returned the morning,
  In the east the light appears;
Golden fringe each cloud adorning;
  Banished all my foolish fears.

So these storm-tossed tides of feeling
  Hear the Saviour's word, "Be still!"
Straight his peace, upon me stealing,
  Quiets my rebellious will.

A NOVEMBER SUNRISE.

RISE at the dawn to see the morning star,
Its brightness scarcely dimmed by wisps of
    cloud
That seek to hide it. Watch those veils of cloud
Their first deep purple hue assume. How calm
They hover o'er the expectant earth,—like wings
Of morning angels, promising the day !
But while we watch they change. From morning's
    brow
The sombre, thoughtful shadow passes off ;
A richer crimson clothes the purple cloud,
And this to joyous scarlet brightens.
Thus, though no living thing be in thy sight,
The landscape wakes to life. Soon leafless
    trees,
And the brown earth herself, break forth in praise
When into burnished gold the scarlet runs,
As the sun rises ; while the stream of light

6

Which from the morning star, a silver thread,
First flowed, then widened in the changing cloud,
Now in a flood of glory, from the sun,
Fills every vale with loveliness, and breaks
In splendor o'er each hilltop, far and near.

A MARCH SUNSET.

I℣ brilliant drapery of the wind-rent clouds,
The Day-King, slow retiring, clothes his throne.
Come to the shelter of yon heavy pines,
And there, defended from the searching gales
Which scarce as yet have checked the furious
    speed
With which the livelong day they 've coursed the
    earth,
Let us enjoy this brilliant sunset scene, —
West, east, north, south, and zenith all alike
Glittering with many-colored fleecy clouds,
Driving like snow-flakes in a stormy wind.

While overhead the herd, with lurid glare,
Seem mad with all the fury of the gale,
A partial quiet in the horizon reigns.
The south, with rosy light piled fleece on fleece;
The north, with gilded snow-banks dazzling bright;

The east, with purple and with violet decked,—
All fade before the glory of the royal west.
There the proud king who rules both winds and
    clouds,
And this day called them to their breathless race,
Is lingering on Wachusett's lofty top
To take a farewell glance o'er his domain
And give his blessing to the wind-vexed land.
Around him brilliant clouds, as vesture flung,
Glow with the glory which his presence gives,
And o'er his head a diadem of rays
Spreads golden splendor o'er a sea of fire.

BEECH HILL.

THE heaven was clothed in leaden gray,
As o'er the hill I took my way;
And keen and chilly was the air
That swept the fields and pastures bare.
My road, a rough and stony path,
Bore scars from many a torrent's wrath,
Which often, on that hillside steep,
Had ploughed their furrows wide and deep.
I went alone; all others sought
The smoother path, more newly wrought,
Which wound about below the hill,
Led by a slowly falling rill;
There alders grew beside the way,
And held the searching wind at bay.

I went alone? No, — one dear Friend,
With me that blessed day to spend,
Was at my side where'er I trod:

Man's truest, nearest friend is God.
His love the grateful cloud had spread,
To guard from midday sun my head;
He fanned me with this cooling air,
That I the toilsome task might bear.
His rains had formed these furrows deep,
In which no searching wind could creep:
In them I sat when weary; there
I asked no sheltering alder's care.
And when I reached the hilltop wild,
A group of pines received his child.
His foresight there a feast had placed
With golden-rod and pearlweed graced.
The pampered sons of wealth might scorn
The fruit of bramble and of thorn;
But blackberry and haw, thus placed,
Were rich as manna to my taste;
And all the hill whereon I trod,
Like Sinai, was the Mount of God.

WATER.

WATER's wonders who has told?
Naught in Nature I behold
Half so Protean in its forms,
Each peculiar in its charms.
Lovely in the placid lake,
Grand where awful surges break;
In the ocean it may be
Type of vast eternity,
In the river's ceaseless flow
Time's perpetual efflux show.
Through the world's unceasing round
Ever active it is found;
Rudest, strongest, in its wrath,
Gentlest in its noiseless path.
Rocks are powerless to withstand
Water with its glacial hand;
Smallest lichen on the stone,
Through the water's aid, has grown;

Tiniest midges o'er it fly,
Draw from water life's supply.
In the Spring, when flowerets burst
From the dark and silent earth,
Each with water slakes its thirst,
Each to water owes its birth.
And in winter, when the sky
Pours down countless graceful flowers,
All the snow-storm's vast supply
Comes from water's magic powers.
Through the cloud of Summer rain
Rises still the sevenfold arch ;
Morn and eve with watery train
Of glory crown the day-king's march.
Every form that water takes
Some new sense of beauty wakes,
Since the day when o'er its face
God's Spirit moved, and left his trace.

TOTUM IN EO.

ALL is in perpetual flow ;
Outward things still come and go ;
Whatsoe'er thy grief to-day,
'T will to-morrow pass away.

Inward gifts alone abide,
Shifting not with wind and tide ;
Only in the constant mind
Thou canst lasting treasure find.

Seek for truth ; pursue her light,
Striving ever for the right ;
Let earth quake, and ocean roar, —
Thou hast peace forevermore.

WALPOLE, N. H.

THOSE Walpole hills! I oft shall roam
  In memory o'er their sunlit sides,
'Neath which, through soft and verdant meads,
  The graceful river slowly glides.

How sweet it was, at early dawn,
  While all about me yet was still,
To watch the fog-bank slowly rise
  And hide the base of every hill.

The village spires, deep in the vale,
  Were floating on a seeming sea;
Nor could Schcherezade's tales
  More fanciful and dreamy be.

The clouds which hovered in the west,
  And hung around each mountain height,
Caught the first rays of rising day,
  And glittered in the purple light.

Like some proud giant in his strength,
　Far to the north, Ascutney stood;
While on his head the opening east
　Poured out of light a golden flood.

To memory's eye, those scenes still shine
　As brightly as when first I saw
The beauty of their wood-crowned hills,
　Or heard the neighboring rapids roar.

Those rapids! oh, what pure delight,
　Reclined upon the rocks to lie, —
An airy bridge above me stretched,
　A foaming torrent rushing by,

Which, as it dashed the rocks among,
　Tossing in air its jewelled spray,
Still uttered, in its thunder-tones,
　A ceaseless anthem, night and day!

That changeless sound a changeless Power,
　Eternal in his being, taught,
Filling the mind with holy awe,
　And upward leading every thought.

THE APOTHEOSIS OF PAN.

But half a man and half a brute,
　A listless satyr wandered,
And all the golden hours of June
　In idle rambles squandered.

While roaming thus ('t was ages since),
　He found, one morning early,
A spot where man, new-comer then
　On earth, was reaping barley.

The satyr paused, and lounging sat
　To view the operation,
And as he sat, played with the straws
　For want of occupation.

But, blowing in the square-cut ends,
　His listlessness soon vanished,
And busy plans of cunning work
　All thoughts of reaping banished.

Before the reapers left the field,
  The satyr had completed
His pipes, and with new melodies
  Their wondering ears had greeted.

They left their sickles in the field,
  And gathered round to hear him;
His wondrous music forces them
  To reverence and fear him.

He seemed at will to swell their hearts
  With sorrow or with pleasure;
Their every passion rose and fell
  Responsive to his measure.

No idle rambler then was he,
  No lounging, useless satyr;
They deified him, — called him Pan,
  A demigod creator.

Thus has it proved a thousand times
  In all succeeding ages,
And seeming trifles still convert
  The seeming fools to sages.

For highest deeds of usefulness,
  When Providence so pleases,
The chance is still to each man sent, —
  Which happy he who seizes!

ODE

FOR LAYING THE CORNER-STONE OF MEMORIAL HALL,

OCTOBER 6, 1870.

OH, holy is the golden light
  Of the October day,
When Summer leaves in dolphin hues
  Of beauty pass away;

But holier the mellow glow
  Fond memory throws around
The names of those whose noble lives
  A noble death has crowned.

More brilliant than on forest trees
  The ripened leaf can be,
The splendor of their glorious deeds
  For God and liberty.

Forever hallowed are these shades
    Where, in the bloom of youth,
They consecrated every power
    To Christ, his Church, and Truth.

And hallowed is their native land,
    For whom their strength they gave
To serve her in her hour of need,
    Then filled the hero's grave.

More lasting than this sacred hall
    Their deathless fame shall be,
Wreathed in a nation's gratitude
    Through all eternity.

DE REPUBLICA BENE SPERAVI.

TEN thousand years ago,
Possibly more (great the uncertainty,
Reading the rock dial of history),
    The earth lay hid in snow;

In mountains skyward piled,
Nearer the pole; sliding thence southerly,
Blasting all life: regions now tropical
    With not a floweret smiled.

The moon looked down and sighed.
"Beautiful earth, dazzling in brilliancy,
Gone are thy flowers, vanished thine animals!
    Though bright, how dark!" she cried.

Those myriad years rolled by.
Melting away, slowly or rapidly,
Mountain of ice, snow-field, and glacier
    Had gone; the earth was dry,

And countless graceful flowers
Sprang from her lap; over her continents
Animals roamed; man, as a sovereign,
    Exulted in his powers.

The moon spake out again :
"Foolish my dream, thinking that history
Closed with the ice; 't was the machinery
    To fit the earth for men. ·

"That awful march of ice,
Rounding the hills, smoothing the plains for them,
Grinding to loam richest materials,
    Has made earth paradise."

SEPTEMBER 12, 1869.

My carpet the fragrant wintergreen,
  My walls with oak and hazel hung,
My ceiling the sky, and lofty pines
  Among whose boughs cicadas sung.

" How frail," I said, " is man's estate !
  How swift our friends are snatched away !
In vain we seek to render aid ;
  They perish ere the close of day."

" Grieve not, O man," the insects sang,
  " Nor mourn the dead ; they live above.
Still let thy heart's unconquered glow
  Be pledge of an immortal love.

" Our seven weeks of life are brief ;
  At earliest touch of frost we die ;
Yet no September night can chill
  Our native fervor of July."

Should man, whom air and seas obey,
    For whom fruits ripen, flowerets bloom,
Who reads all Nature's language, dread
    The short-lived winter of the tomb?

All beauty in the earth or sky,
    All love that holiest hearts can know,
Are but faint images which strive
    The eternal love of God to show.

RESURGET.

THE pallid leaf floats from the tree,
  And fading joys flit from my heart;
  Dull pains record that they depart;
The account is left with grief and me.

Grief madly whispers: "He has fled,
  As withering leaves float from the tree;
  In Nature's course, they cease to be;
And who shall wake the slumbering dead?"

The brave heart answers: "Leaves may fall,
  Return again to parent earth,
  And give new generations birth;
None ask their beauties to recall."

Not so with him whom I have wept,
  With those who mourn for him with me:
  We cannot hold that death may be,
But know that he has only slept.

Faith is the proof of things not seen.
Since He is true who fills the heart
With faith and hope, I cannot part
From my fixed trust; on Him I lean.

SPRINGTIME.

AGAIN the northward climbing sun
The mid-point of his path hath won,
And bluebirds, softly warbling, bring
The early promise of the spring.

I share their hope, I share their joy;
I would in praise my song employ;
Yet, ah! the bluebird ne'er can know
My springtime memories of woe.

Nine winters' melting ice and snow
Have swelled, each March, Neponset's flow,
Since that sad springtime when we laid
His form beneath the pine-trees' shade.

Although the bluebirds yearly sing,
And flowers adorn returning spring,
No south wind's warm and fragrant breath
Can loose the icy chains of death.

Yet still my heart will whisper low:
"The deeper piled is winter's snow,
And longer felt his icy powers,
The brighter bloom the vernal flowers."

TO AN ANTIOPA.

WANDERER with me in this sunlight,
    Art thou sharer of my joy?
Do such thronging hopes and memories
    Form thy fancy's sweet employ?

Thou, as I, hast tasted pleasure;
    Thou, with me, hast suffered pain:
We have both survived a winter;
    Spring revives us both again.

But thy winter only witnessed
    The moon six times her courses run;
The stormy clouds of mine outmeasured
    Thrice the circuit of the sun!

Thine was passed in torpid slumber,
    Pain or fear thou didst not know;
Mine, mid frequent fears and anguish, —
    Agony in every throe.

But thy joy, renewed in sunshine,
  Soon in endless death shall close;
Mine the sun himself outlasteth, —
  Death my being never knows.

Such the all-wise Father's pleasure:
  Highest good we reach through pain;
Half the joy of April's sunshine
  Comes from cold December's rain.

REALITIES.

OH, never deem this world a dream
Of things which are not what they seem!
For He who hurled through space this world,
And the starry skies above unfurled,
Can never lie; and earth and sky
Are what he wrote for the human eye.
The fool, indeed, or child, may read
Only the letters, with careless heed;
And fail to see what mystery
Contained in the sacred whole may be.
But he whose sight is open to light
Finds the page with heavenly glories bright.
Yet the clearest ray of the infinite day,
Through this elder Scripture beaming alway,
Gives the steadfast hope that there yet shall ope
On our stronger vision a wider scope;
When, through Christ's grace, we face to face
Shall see what passeth all time and space.

Then the brightest gleam of the present shall seem
Mere darkness beside that immortal beam.

But the present glow is bright also
With the glories of heaven that round us flow.
For on Nature's face we can clearly trace
The tokens of Godhead in every place.
In every line God's power divine,
His love and wisdom, steadily shine;
In his hand we lie, while with raptured eye
We read his truth on earth and sky.

CHICKADEE.

THE song-sparrow has a joyous note,
  The brown thrush whistles bold and free;
But my little singing-bird at home
  Sings a sweeter song to me.

The catbird, at morn or evening, sings
  With liquid tones, like gurgling water;
But sweeter by far, to my fond ear,
  Is the voice of my little daughter.

Four years and a half since she was born,
  The black-caps piping cheerily;
And so, as she came in winter with them,
  We have called her our Chickadee.

She sings to her dolls, she sings alone,
  And singing round the house she goes;
Out-doors or within, her happy heart
  With a childlike song o'erflows.

Her mother and I, though busy, hear,
  With mingled pride and pleasure listening ;
And thank the inspiring Giver of song,
  While a tear in our eye is glistening.

Oh, many a bird of sweetest song
  I hear when in woods or meads I roam ;
But sweeter by far than all, to me,
  Is my Chickadee at home.

TO THE CATBIRD.

BESIDE the lovely Raritan,
That quaintly carves its red-shale cliffs,
My childhood's ear drank in thy song,
Ere yet my childish heart could know
How rich the content of the lay.
But fifty years of life may teach
The dullest scholar how to hear
And see, to understand and feel.
Now, in the valley of the Charles,
Thy song familiar lifts the veil;
I see more plainly, and I hear
More clearly what I heard in youth.
Thy melodies then filled my heart
With childlike happiness, and gave
An added pleasure to the hours
Of boyish idleness or play;
But now they rouse the deepest thoughts
And holiest feelings of my soul, —

Reverence and faith and gratitude.
I doubt not that thy song is tuned
To please thyself and please thy mate;
And yet I doubt if you or she
Can feel its meaning as I feel.
More thoughtful than the bobolink,
More joyous than the oriole,
Its liquid warblings speak, to me,
Of sweet contentment born of faith;
Of happiness not thoughtless, stayed
On wisdom, nurtured still by love.
Surely, sweet bird, thy voice, thus rich
In meanings far beyond thy ken,
Is utterance of a higher soul,
Which speaks through thee to human hearts.
Thy song has thus a double sense, —
Bearing one meaning to thy mate,
A higher meaning to our ears:
One meaning thine, for her to feel;
The other, His who bade thee sing,
And taught our human hearts to feel the song.

THE BROWN THRUSH.

HARK! the brown thrush in the tree
To his mate is singing!
With the music of the tale
All the woodland ringing!

Dainty bits to feed their young
He has just been bringing;
Now pours out his happy heart,
On the elm-branch swinging.

THE SEAL.

HERE in my newly planted tree,
Ere its leaves open to the sun,
A bird begins to weave its nest:
Thus God accepts the work I 've done.

8

WASHINGTON.

GREATEST is he who serves most willingly,
And shows most wisdom in the way he serves.
Service which flows from love, not from constraint,
Wisely directed, not with blundering haste,
Alone is noble, and alone is life.
For love and wisdom are such attributes
As show a man to be inspired from Heaven;
They lift him into fellowship with God.
Thus saith that ancient seer whose eagle eye
Pierced through the seventh heaven, who also
    heard
The mystic sound of the Eternal Word.

The fount of being is immortal love;
Not idle passion, such as poets sing,
But that unmeasured goodness whose sole aim
Is but the highest good of all. All draw
From Him the stream of being and of life;

But he whose law of action and of thought
Is still in unison with that high end
Becomes thereby partaker in the life
Which knows no bounds of space or time or power.
Such men alone we truly can call great,
Serving by deed or word, in Church or State.

And he is least who seeks most zealously
Himself to exalt, to serve his private ends.
All his success is transient; it must lead
Only to ruin and oblivion.
The envious men who carped at Washington,
Or fain would build their fortunes on his fall,
Themselves have faded into nothingness;
While he who lived for public ends alone,
Whose wisdom, goodness, strength, were all engaged
In the continual service of his race,
Takes in the ranks of fame the highest place.

THE SHIP OF STATE.

MARCH, 1865.

FIERCELY the raging billows
Toss the good ship; breakers ahead
Roar with hoarse, loud threats, and the wind
 Shrieks in the cordage wildly.

Not that the tempest only
Made us shrink, fear-struck, but the crew
Left their posts each one, and began
 Angry and loud debating.

Thanks unto Him who ruleth
Over e'en men's hearts, that the crew,
Ere the fierce waves swallowed the ship,
 Turned them again to duty!

Yet is the tempest raging!
Now may God give, Captain, to thee
Heart to stand firm, skill to avoid
 Shipwreck for four years longer!

FLAG OF FREEDOM.

STARS! whose lustre evermore is beaming, —
'Neath the noonday, when the moon is gleaming,
In the darkest night the brightest seeming, —
  Glowing in the sunniest hour!
Glorious stripes! as ruddy as the dawning, —
Ever floating in eternal morning,
Thus our skies with beauty still adorning,
    Whether suns may shine or tempests grimly
      lower!

Flag of freedom! grandly waving o'er us,
Guide us still, whatever be before us,
While we swear, as now, in solemn chorus,
  Foe nor traitor thee shall harm.
When dark clouds on the horizon lower,
When the thunder tells the tempest's power,
War's alarums threatening every hour,
    Thoughts of thee shall warm each heart and
      nerve each arm.

Flag of freedom! grandly wave forever!
Guard our coasts, protect each lake and river,
Crown each hill, illume each vale, and never
   Let one stripe or star grow dim.
When our sires, with love of freedom glowing,
Took up arms, full well the danger knowing,
God blessed then the seed which they were sowing.
   Still may he protect their sons! We trust in him.

CHRISTMAS.

In a manger, on the hay,
Mary's new-born infant lay ;
Though the child was fair and sweet,
Yet its helplessness complete.

But that Power which called the light
Out of chaos' rayless night,
And around our new-made world
Rolling suns and systems hurled,
Chose that through this infant's eyes
Brighter daybreaks should arise ;
Chose that by this gentle hand
Mightier force at his command
Should new heavens and earth create.
Only thirty years to wait,
 And those silent lips shall say
Words that cannot pass away.
From that humble village inn,

Lo! a movement shall begin,
Through the coming ages roll,
And the world at length control.

Men who saw this infant son
In the streets of Nazareth run
Lived to mourn his early loss
When he died upon the cross;
Lived till his victorious foes
Drank, defeated, bitter woes;
Till the blood ran, bridle-deep,
Down Moriah's hillside steep;
Till the Roman eagles soared
Where the storm of battle roared;
Till the smoke of sacrifice
Had forever ceased to rise;
When the temple, stone by stone,
Scattered lay, all overthrown.

Men who saw this victim die
By the cross on Calvary
Lived until the cross became
Badge of glory, not of shame,
To a still increasing host,

On each near and distant coast.
Then this mightier force began
Further conquests over man, —
Not to enslave, but to set free;
Lifting into liberty,
Slaying cruelty and lust,
Humbling tyrants to the dust,
Giving victory to the just,
Making still the meek and pure
Heirs to wealth that shall endure.

As the mighty cedars rise,
Slow and silent, toward the skies,
Thus the influence of this child
Through the ages, sweet and mild,
Lifted still our fallen race
Toward the vision of God's face.

Five-and-twenty centuries
Since Isaiah's prophecies,
Yet his words each day appear
More and more divinely clear.
Mary's Son the pledge redeems;
'T is from him the radiance streams,

Where in darkness nations walked,
And the awful spectres stalked,
Bred by ignorance and fear.
'T is his kingdom, drawing near,
Loosed the fetters from the slave,
Freedom to the captive gave,
And the garments, rolled in blood,
Gives the fire to be its food.
To this Son the power is given
Over things on earth, in heaven.
His dominion, oh, how great!
Nations bow before his feet!
Over sin the conqueror!
Wonderful and Counsellor!
Founder of a future age,
Boundless is his heritage!

In a manger, on the hay,
Mary's new-born infant lay:
Angels welcomed then his birth,
Coming to redeem the earth.
We would echo now their song,
And their notes of praise prolong.
Holy child, so fair and sweet,

May thy triumph be complete!
May thy lovely, spotless youth,
May thy words of living truth,
May thy life in Galilee,
And thy death on Calvary
Draw at length all hearts to thee!

THE NATIVITY.

" Infancy is a perpetual Messiah."

O SINLESS brother of our sinful race !
How easy, now, thy horoscope to trace!
But when a babe at Mary's side, new-born,
Who could forecast the day from such a morn ?
That voice, — a wailing infant's feeble breath, —
Shall that e'er heal the sick, or raise from death ?
Or shall that form, which now so helpless lies,
Triumphant leave the tomb and seek the skies ?
That humble name, now only heard at home,
Be heard with awe far as imperial Rome
Extends her vast domains ?   And shall it claim
To be exalted over every name ?

That claim long since was granted; every tongue
Thee, as the only Lord, has daily sung ;
While saint and sinner have alike confessed

In thee their hope, through thee their prayers
    addressed.
Still may thy power subdue thy foes, until
All hearts are melted, sanctified each will,
Our sinful race redeemed, to life restored;
Till man by righteousness shall praise his Lord.

Though only once in all the lapse of time
Appeared on earth his majesty sublime,
In all things like his brethren, it is said,
That merciful and faithful priest was made, —
His life the type and pattern for our race,
Toward which he leads us by indwelling grace.
Thus would I find, sweet Mary's babe, in thee
A type of every human infancy.
Whene'er a house an infant may contain,
It might be called a beth-lehem again.
Though Judah's hamlet best deserves that name,
Since there from Heaven's abounding wealth there
    came
That Bread which gives to him who eats thereof
Eternal life, — a life of light and love, —
Yet living bread, in humbler measure given,
Is sent with every babe. It comes from Heaven,

And kindles life and light and love in them
Who dwell around its little Bethlehem.

And who can tell its future? Who shall say
What work may burden, and what crown its day?
The glory God gave him, our Saviour said,
He gave to those who, by the Spirit led,
Believed on him through his apostles' word, —
That is, the countless host who own him Lord.
For greater works, he promised, they should do
Than he had done. And doubtless he who knew
What was in man foresaw the coming age, —
The boundless riches of man's heritage,
The endless opportunity to be
Co-laborers with God whenever we
A fellow-man whom we can serve may see.

A child that's born to-day may one day rise
Leader in counsel, great in enterprise,
A glorious benefactor to his race;
A priest at Nature's altar, skilled to trace
The wondrous order of creation's plan;
An artist who by inspiration can
Proclaim through form or color, or through tone,

The evangel of God's love through beauty shown.
And should the new-born infant ne'er attain
To earthly power or honors, but remain
Unknown, unnoticed, who shall dare to say
His life has been a blank, a failure? Nay!
The Prince of Light, who has redeemed the world,
And from his throne the Prince of Darkness hurled,
Was crucified between two thieves, and left
His friends disheartened, of all hope bereft.
His life appeared a failure. Those who thought
He was the Son of David, and had brought
Deliverance to Israel, sunk in gloom,
Buried all hope with him in Joseph's tomb.

And many a follower of the Crucified,
Unknown, unnoticed by the living tide
Which flowed around, has firmly placed his feet
Upon the rock, has boldly dared to meet
The dangers, sufferings, and toils of life,
And Satan's wiles, a hero in the strife.
Unknown? Unnoticed? No! the All-seeing Eye,
Unmarked by whom a sparrow cannot die,
Marks well his humblest effort to obey
The royal law, while Jesus, day by day,

Sustains with hidden manna, and bestows
A final victory over all his foes.
And men who noted not this neighbor's power
Were, without noting, influenced every hour.
The skill divine which by the dreadful cross
Restored the fallen world from Eden's loss,
Knows well how humblest agent, in his hand,
May do the mightiest works at his command.

How dear that scene which Mark for us portrays!
Jesus takes infants in his arms, and lays
His hand in blessing on their heads; declares
The childlike man alone God's kingdom shares.
O sinless brother of our sinful race!
Divinest gift of God's unmeasured grace!
Still may the spirit of a childlike love
And manly faith, combined, forever prove
That we have been with thee, and learned to know
What inward peace Hope, Faith, and Love bestow;
Faith which sees God in every child appear,
And Love which treats all men as brethren dear.

THE RESURRECTION.

WHILE yet the western heavens were all aglow
With lingering steps of day, the full-orbed moon
Rose slowly o'er the heights of Olivet;
The Sabbath stillness had not passed away.
The guilty city, which the day before
Exulted in the murder of the Just,
Lay hushed in moonlight. Through its lonely streets
But few were moving. On its level roofs
Reclining groups held converse with the stars,
Or in hushed whispers spoke of Jesus' death.
"Might it not be," some asked, "he was, as claimed
By fond disciples, Israel's rightful king?
'T was said, indeed, that at the judgment bar
Of Pilate he had owned he was a king.
Perchance his taking off was treason's act,
Which must bring judgment down from righteous
      Heaven.

9

This moonlight stillness, — was it but the lull
Which presages the tempest's awful wrath?"
And still they dared not answer, to themselves,
The questions which they asked.

       The night wore on;
The moon at length rode down the western sky,
And feverish watchers scanned the eastern hills
With longing for the earliest glimpse of dawn.
Then from the northern gate two women steal,
To seek, alone, the spot where Jesus lies.
His sacred body they would still embalm
With spice and nard, and with affection's tears.
Soon, hastily returning, they arouse
The impetuous Peter and the ardent John.
The four go back to seek the garden grave.
The sepulchre no longer holds its dead!
The women weep that sacrilegious hands
Have robbed the tomb; the men go in the cave.
There lies the napkin, here the linen cloth, —
The cerements which had wrapped the holy clay, —
But that which they had held was gone!
Then John and Peter, wondering at the theft,
And wondering that the thieves had left the
  cloths,

Return with one companion, leaving there
Mary, who stands and still in silence weeps.

Oh, grateful heart! what strong affection beats
In every pulse that shakes her heaving breast!
Oh, grateful heart! what treasures shall be thine!
What honors that shall be vouchsafed to thee,
To thee alone! Thou art the first to know
That fact which soon the Roman Empire raised
From its abyss of sin; yea, all the world.
Lo! thine arisen Lord has deigned to come,
To still with tender words thine anxious fear,
And give thee peace. "Why weepest thou?" he
      asks.
But she, half blind with tears (while yet nor moon,
Descending low, nor dawn, was giving light),
First peered within the tomb, and angels saw;
Then thought the gardener had approached the
      spot.
A third time Jesus speaks, and calls her name.
Her name, thus spoken, thrills through all her
      soul;
Her sense is opened, and she knows her Lord.
The tide of feeling, suddenly thus turned

From grief to joy, tumultuously rolls
Within her heart, and its own utterance chokes;
But, falling at his feet, she simply cries,
" My Master!"
                    He replied, " Detain me not!
Go, tell my brethren I will meet them soon."
She, still bewildered, goes to tell the tale
To those who saw with her the empty tomb.
From mouth to mouth the rapid tidings fly.
The faithful friends of Jesus hear with hope;
His foes, with unbelief, yet trembling fear.
Day wore away, and later moonrise left
A transient darkness; ten of those whom he
Had chosen from the rest in secret meet,
To talk of Mary's news or question her.
Lo! when the doors were shut, himself was there!
All stand amazed; while he, in gentle tones,
Bestows his blessing, bids them all behold
His wounded hands and side, and then receive
His last commission, take the keys of power,
And bear the gospel forth through every land.

Oh, ne'er before nor since have words so sweet
Borne fruit so rich, produced effect so great!

Henceforth shall Peter well deserve his name,
Nor maiden's taunts make him deny his Lord;
No longer, at the sight of Roman guards,
Basely shall all forsake the Crucified.
But that new life which in the garden tomb
Brought forth the Conqueror in immortal strength,
Now lives in all the ten; its floods shall rise
And flow through every land, through every age,
Giving all nations an eternal Spring.
'T was in the Spring-time God from Egypt called
His chosen race; 't was Spring-time when he raised
From death's Egyptian darkness his dear Son.
The ten, in deep amaze but holy joy,
Receive his parting charge; he then departs.
And when their swelling hearts an utterance found,
The first glad Easter hymn as incense rose to God.

    From the midnight of the grave,
    All victorious, strong to save,
    Comes, refulgent as the sun,
    Jesus, God's anointed One.

    Darkness he has driven away;
    He has brought immortal day;

Death and Hades strive in vain
Night and chaos to retain.

Hail, thou Mighty Conqueror,
Wonderful and Counsellor,
Lord of glory, Prince of peace!
Never shall thine empire cease.

Jesus, from among the dead,
Raises his triumphant head;
Sing the glad, exultant strain,
Hell is conquered, Death is slain!

LO–NEHUSHTAN.

THEY grieve my heart, — these thoughtless men
    who try
  To hide my Lord from eyes of dying men;
  To shroud the world in heathen night again,
And drag the Star of Bethlehem from the sky.

They hold his majesty a vain pretence;
  They snatch the royal sceptre from his hand,
  Deny his right to promise or command,
And barely own his human excellence.

Therefore I weep, like Mary, at his grave,
Because my Lord they thus have borne away,
  To hide him from the eyes of dying men.
  Yet he has risen now, as he had then;
Look up in faith! His light outshines the day;
His grace is still omnipotent to save.

THE EVERLASTING LIGHT.

ALL-HOLY, ever-living One,
  With uncreated splendor bright!
Darkness may blot from heaven the sun, —
  Thou art my everlasting light.

Let every star withhold its ray,
  Clouds hide the earth and sky from sight;
Fearless I still pursue my way
  Toward thee, my everlasting light.

Thou art the only source of day;
  Forgetting thee alone is night;
All things for which we hope or pray
  Flow from thine everlasting light.

Still nearer thee my soul would rise;
  Thus she attains her highest flight,
And, as the eagle sunward flies,
  Seeks thee, her everlasting light.

"COME UNTO ME."

THE night was dark; the winds were high,
  Which landward drove the roaring sea.
I knew a rocky coast was nigh;
  I saw not how from death to flee.

Then, mid the gloom, I heard a voice:
  "Come unto me," it sweetly said.
At first, scarce daring to rejoice,
  I toward the speaker turned my head.

No form was seen the waters o'er;
  Yet once again that voice I heard,
Sweet sounding o'er the breakers' roar;
  Then I obeyed the sovereign word.

When, lo! a gleaming path appeared,
  Leading within a sheltered bay;
With desperate strength my course I steered,
  To keep that straight and narrow way.

Then soon behind the rocks, at ease,
    The Hand which placed them there I blessed ;
Thus shielding me from stormy seas,
    Thus letting me securely rest.

Should e'er again the storm grow wild,
    And dangers gather round my way,
I 'll hearken for those accents mild,
    " Come unto me," and will obey.

THE HEAVENLY GUEST.

I HEAR a gentle tapping at the door.
    Be still, my soul! and listen to the word
Of Him who knocks and pleadeth evermore
    For entrance; 't is thy Saviour and thy Lord.

Oh, why so slow in answering his call?
    Why thus reluctant to admit thy guest?
All springs of happiness are scant and small
    Beside his loving presence in the breast.

'T is love alone which brings him to thy door;
    'T was love divine which sent him unto men;
'T is pardon, peace, and joy forevermore
    He freely gives. Refuse him not again.

Oh, quickly open at his gracious call,
    And gladly welcome so divine a guest!
Return thy love for his: the gift is small;
    While he gives bliss untold, and endless rest.

EPXOT, KTPIE.

Yea, come, dear Lord! My heart
　I fain would open wide
For thee to enter; nor depart,
　But with me to abide.

Abide with me; and teach
　My feeble heart to know
How to thy stature I may reach,
　To perfect manhood grow.

I hear thee knock without,
　Seeking to enter in;
And yet I suffer fear and doubt
　To keep me in my sin, —

The sins of unbelief,
　Distrust, and cowardice,
Which cause my gracious Saviour grief;
　Nor will they let me rise.

Oh, could I rise above
  These earth-born mists, and see
The heaven of thine unclouded love,
  And dwell therein with thee!

My heart I long to find
  Freed from its selfish care,
Filled with pure love to all mankind,
  With faith and hope, with prayer.

Therefore to thee I fly ;
  Dwell thou within my breast !
Weary and heavy-laden, I
  In thee alone find rest.

THE CRUCIFIXION.

O HOLY Lamb of God!
　　Must thou to slaughter go,
And on thy sinless shoulders bear
　　Our heritage of woe?

Must thou endure our grief,
　　Our stripes be laid on thee?
The sins of many must thou take,
　　And thus our ransom be?

What depth of wondrous love
　　Could lead thee thus to die,
The garden and the cross to meet,
　　For sinners such as I?

Oh, take my stubborn heart,
　　And mould it at thy will!
Thy love makes rebel pride submit,
　　And passion's tempest still.

A THANKSGIVING.

PRAISE to Him, all praise excelling,
Who, in light eternal dwelling,
Hears the immortal chorus swelling
   From all creatures to his praise.
Thanks to him for our creation,
For the offers of salvation;
Every tribe and every nation
   Songs of honor gladly raise.

Who his bounties e'er could measure, —
Tell out Nature's endless treasure,
Count up every source of pleasure,
   All his wondrous gifts rehearse?
Earth, with all her fruits and flowers,
Mines of wealth, and secret powers,
Quickening sun, refreshing showers, —
   Earth transcends the power of verse.

But a soul with rapture glowing,
Or a heart with love o'erflowing,
Peace inbreathed from Heaven thus knowing, —
   This transcends all joys of earth.
Thou whose bounties none can measure,
Give us this, the gospel treasure, —
This divine, immortal pleasure,
   Of eternal, priceless worth.

Then to thee, for our creation,
For the gospel's free salvation,
Sent through Christ to every nation,
   We our joyful thanks will raise,
Still the theme the heavens be telling;
Seraphim, upon it dwelling,
Still the immortal chorus swelling,
   Fill eternity with praise.

CHEERFUL PRAISE.

YE sons of Zion, sing
With cheerful heart and voice
The praises of your heavenly King,
And in his love rejoice.

The living stones are ye,
Of which his house is built;
From sin his Christ has set you free,
And cleansed you from your guilt.

He called you from the night
In which all nations lay,
And floods you with the wondrous light
Of his eternal day.

Show forth his praise in song,
In holiness and love ;
Through earthly years the strain prolong,
Through countless years above.

10

JERUSALEM.

Jerusalem ! Oh, sacred name,
  How rich in holy memories !
The brutal Roman quenched the flame
  Which lit her daily sacrifice ;
But memory still delights to dwell
  Upon the earlier, purer days
When prophets' words like manna fell,
  And Zion's courts were filled with praise.

The new Jerusalem ! That word
  Awakes our holiest hope and prayer ;
The promise seems too long deferred,
  Yet faith will cast on God its care.
The dawning light already gleams,
  And calls for songs of grateful praise ;
We hail with joy its earliest beams,
  And loud our hallelujahs raise.

O city of our God, descend!
 As John in holy vision saw;
Our anarchy and darkness end
 In light and liberty and law.
God and the Lamb shall be our light,
 From doubt and error making free;
God's will, to our illumined sight,
 Shall law and life and rapture be.

THE ETERNAL JOY.

O THOU whose boundless power and love
Still with unerring wisdom move,
And, thy grand purpose to fulfil,
Command creation at thy will,

What duty or what bliss have I,
But trustful in thy hand to lie ?
My only strength and wisdom, Lord,
Are strict obedience to thy word.

Let not my wayward passions draw
My rebel heart to hate thy law,
But let almighty grace control
To sweet submission all my soul.

The joys and comforts I have known
Flowed from thy bounteous hand alone ;
Let all my hope and longing be
To find forever joy in thee.

MOODS.

Look ! how these snow-clad fields throw back,
  Unmoved, the quickening noontide ray ;
Nor life nor motion in their clods,
  Or rests by night, or wakes by day.

My heart is ice ; its tides are stilled
  Beneath the deep and crusted snow ;
Like half-forgotten dreams appear
  The hallowed moods I used to know.

But when three moons have passed, these fields
  Shall feel the south wind's gentle breath,
Unlock their treasures, and give proof
  How real is life, how seeming death.

O gentler Spirit from above,
  When shall this torpid bosom know
The influence of thy holy breath,
  From which faith, love, and courage flow ?

OUT OF THE DEPTHS.

O GOD! mine agony is great,
  Yet thine the hand that struck the blow;
Help me in patient hope to wait
  Till thy full purpose I may know.

I know thou dost not wound in vain;
  For thou art love, and changest not:
Thou sendest both the joy and pain
  That vary still my earthly lot.

I think of dread Gethsemane,
  Of all my Saviour's anguish there;
And then the burden laid on me
  Becomes as light as Summer air.

JOYOUS SUBMISSION.

O God! mine eyes and ears unseal
   To see thine angels ever near,
And hear their voices; may I feel
   Nor rebel pride nor slavish fear.

I bless thee for the holy joys
   Thy grace has taught my glowing heart;
Henceforth thy will be all my choice;
   I could not choose a better part.

Each dearest hope, each anxious fear,
   My fondest longings, I would still;
I lay them on thine altar here,
   And only seek to do thy will.

IMMANUEL'S LAND.

O FATHER! cleanse our inmost souls
   By thine almighty grace, and fill
Our hearts with burning zeal and power
   To learn and do thy holy will.
Form Christ within us; let us live
The life which thou through him shalt give.

Oh, let our land, which thou hast blest
   Above all other lands, receive
Thy greatest gift, that quickening grace
   Through which thy trusting saints believe.
Let antichrist and sin be slain,
And Christ in every bosom reign.

Make thou our land Immanuel's land!
   Be thou our everlasting light,
Our sun that nevermore shall set,
   With uncreated glory bright.
Let all our people righteous be,
And find eternal life in thee.

IN HIS NAME.

LIGHT of the world! upon our land
  Thy glorious splendors shine;
Let not our foolish eyes be closed
  Against the light divine.

Nor let us basely be content
  Ourselves to use the ray,
While wandering thousands fail to find
  The straight and narrow way.

Light of the world! in our dead hearts
  Shine at this hallowed hour,
To kindle there a living flame
  Of light and love and power.

With lives of purity and zeal,
  With words inspired by thee,
We would, in drawing men to God,
  O Christ, thy servants be.

PATIENT FAITH.

O God ! thy wisdom cannot err,
 Thy tender mercy never fails,
Although thou mayst the help defer
 Till hands and feet are pierced with nails.

Thy Best-belovèd bore the cross ;
 He died that awful death for me :
Help me for him to suffer loss,
 Like him to bear my agony.

Teach me to look in faith to him :
 His wounded feet and hands and side
Have made all earthly honors dim,
 While pain and grief are glorified.

Give me, O Father, strength to bear
 All burdens gladly for his sake ;
With him in grief below to share,
 And in his joys above partake.

DEDICATION AT WALPOLE, N. H.

BEGIRT with wood-crowned hills,
  In loveliness arrayed,
This vale, a temple built by God,
  Was for his worship made.

The birds at early dawn
  To him their matins raise;
The water's roar at evening brings
  Its vesper hymn of praise.

While Nature lifts its voice,
  We would not silent be;
But gladly, Lord, these walls we raise,
  In which to worship thee.

Here let the holy font,
  The supper's sacred rite,
The living word, thy truth, impart
  Their sanctifying light.

With thine own presence, Lord
This house forever bless,
While men shall own thy sovereign grace,
And faith in Christ confess.

EASTER.

ETERNAL Father! at whose word
    Creation flashed to instant birth,
Thy will, which gave this body life,
    Bids it return to lifeless earth!

But thou didst send that risen Lord,
    Who once in Joseph's garden lay,
Burst from the night of transient death,
    And poured on us immortal day.

In his dear name we ask thy help
    By faith in him to live and die;
That, when this body sleeps in dust,
    We may with him ascend on high.

Eternal Father! by thy word
    Raise us from sin, and death's dark night;
That we may even now, with Christ,
    Dwell in the realms of heavenly light!

LUX E TENEBRIS.

FROM the grave in Joseph's garden,
   Where the murdered Saviour lay,
Burst the resurrection's morning,
   Pledging us eternal day.

From the tomb of faithful martyrs,
   And from lips of dying saints,
Flows the Christian's light in darkness, —
   Hope and comfort when he faints.

And 't is thus that fallen heroes
   Bless the land they died to save.
Lo! the light of peace and freedom,
   Streaming from the patriot's grave!

LIGHT AND LIFE.

FROM the dark abyss of being,
  Through the present's narrow strait,
To the abyss of death returning,
  Bearing all its varied freight,
Flows the stream of life, apparent
  Only thus 'twixt death and birth, —
Into darkness never ending
  Sweeping all the sons of earth.

No! a light illumes that darkness :
  Christ has driven its shades away ;
Those through faith in him abiding
  Dwell in everlasting day.
From his opened tomb the splendor
  Of eternal glory pours ;
Through the tomb he leads believers
  Into heaven's unfolding doors.

ADVENT.

WHERE holy Luke the scene has drawn,
  How fair the simple picture stands !
That wayside inn at Bethlehem,
  The helpless babe by loving hands
Within a humble manger laid,
  And Christ, of lowly virgin born,
Announced by angels to the swains
  Who watched their flocks at early morn !

His second advent still the Church
  Looks in the clouds of heaven to see ;
The signs of his approach they wait,
  When in his Father's glory he
Shall come with outward pomp and show,
  While throngs of angels, hovering round,
Arrayed in glittering robes of white,
  Are marshalled to the trumpet's sound.

Come thus or not ; but come, dear Lord !
Within our hearts thy throne maintain ;
In us, and by us, over sin
   The everlasting victory gain !
Thy word, the trumpet ; truth, the light ;
   All creatures, ministers for thee ;
And nations brought beneath thy sway
   Thy clouds of witnesses shall be.

THE SINLESS SUFFERER.

BEHOLD the holy Lamb of God!
His grief and sorrows who can tell?
The chastisement which guilt deserves
Upon his sinless shoulders fell.

How dark the mystery of thy ways,
O God! beyond our mortal ken, —
To send such sorrows on thy Son,
To show such love to guilty men!

When, wrung with anguish, Jesus kneeled,
He said: "Thy will, not mine, be done!"
Thus, when our hours of darkness come,
Help us to pray as prayed thy Son.

Thy will, O God! not ours, be done!
Thou art all-holy, thou all-wise;
Thou knowest wherefore thou hast laid
Through grief the pathway to the skies.

AVE! VIVENS HOSTIA.

SLAIN before eternity,
  Evermore thou livest;
Through thy final sacrifice
  Life to all thou givest.

To the Father ceaselessly
  Thanks and praise we render;
He has made thee be to us
  Saviour, guide, defender.

Bringing life to dying men
  While to death thou goest,
Pardon, peace, and holiness
  Thou on us bestowest.

Hail, thou great reality!
  Mighty still to save us;
Living water, bread of life,
  Which the Father gave us!

THE LIGHT OF LIFE.

THE moon was sinking in the west, —
    Not yet the dawn foretold the day, —
When love's last tribute to their Lord
    The faithful women came to pay.

Lo ! in the darkness then a ray
    Broke from the tomb, so dazzling bright
Their eyes were blinded ; and they fled,
    Not knowing wherefore, in their fright.

Recovering sight, they henceforth walked
    Secure, illumined by that ray ;
Its holy light dispelled the shades,
    And made for them eternal day.

Down through the ages have its beams,
    Amid the darkness, shone serene ;
The way to truth, to life, to God,
    By them alone is truly seen.

CHRIST OUR LIFE.

CONQUEROR of death ! thy mighty voice
  Calls from their graves the sleeping dead !
In that glad sound would I rejoice,
  And lift with theirs my fallen head.

Life without love, I find, is death ;
  Love is not love, which loves not thee :
Both love and life flow from thy breath ;
  Breathe thou both life and love in me !

Thy sacrifice upon the cross
  Has shown the omnipotence of love ;
Our life we gain through thy life's loss,
  Through thy descent we rise above.

From God the fountain, the full stream
  Of life, redundant, flows through thee ;
From him light's uncreated beam
  Shines through thy face eternally.

How deep and tender, wise and strong,
Is his, the all-embracing love,
Which leads through thee our souls along
Toward endless light and life above!

EASTER CAROL.

Who is this with mighty power
From the tomb awaking,
Shaking off the chains of Death,
All his fetters breaking?
Day had not yet dawned when he,
Bursting from his prison,
Shed a million-fold more light
Than the sun when risen.

Death himself he has destroyed,
Fear has turned to gladness,
Tears has wiped from every eye,
Banished all our sadness.
When our friends are called away,
He restrains our weeping;
Those who die in him, he says,
Are but sweetly sleeping.

Who is this ?   The Son of God !
　Jesus, Lord of glory !
Sing his praise forevermore,
　Tell his wondrous story !
When the world in darkness lay,
　Sunk in sin and sorrow,
He from realms of endless day
　Brought the eternal morrow !

EVANGELISTS.

THE whispering sea, the thundering surf,
 The peaceful vale, the craggy height,
The wind, the storm, the darkening cloud,
 And heaven's all-glorious orbs of light, —
These are thy ministers, O God!
These are the preachers of thy Word.

But not through these alone thy words
 Our drowsy souls to life awake;
The eternal Word, thy truth and light,
 Through Jesus' lips and actions break;
We would with love and reverence hear,
And in obedient faith draw near.

O Father! fill the hearts of those
 Who speak in Jesus' holy name,
With all the power of truth and love, —
 With love like that in which he came
To hang on Calvary's awful tree
And draw our conquered hearts to thee!

HERALDS.

" Lo ! I send you," saith the Lord,
   " Bearing tidings glad to men ;
Messages of pardoning love,
   Eden's loss restored again.

" Fountains opened, in whose floods
   Men may wash away their stains ;
Those who drink the healing stream
   Find new life in all their veins."

Fear not, heralds of the cross !
   Faithful to your message prove,
Not ashamed to own your Lord,
   Still rejoicing in his love.

Let him all your wisdom be,
   Serving him your strength employ ;
Souls redeemed from death shall then
   Through all ages be your joy.

FOR AN ORDINATION.

O THOU whose Spirit Moses did inspire,
And touched the prophets' lips with holy fire,
But brightest glowed in Jesus Christ, our Lord,
The midday glory of the eternal Word,

With heavenly light thy servant here inspire!
Touch thou his lips with true prophetic fire!
Teach him to utter boldly all thy Word,
Yet meekly follow his ascended Lord!

That from his lips the glowing truth may burn
Deep in our hearts, to life our deadness turn;
And by his guidance led, at length may we
Come to the fold of Christ, to heaven, and thee!

"THY KINGDOM COME."

Our Father! thou the distant spheres,
    And earth and sea, alike dost hold, —
Their Lord to everlasting years,
    As from eternity of old.

All creatures move but at thy will:
    Thy wisdom guides them, great and small;
The power which made upholds them still;
    Thy kingdom ruleth over all.

Yet feeble man may close his heart
    Against thine omnipresence; raise
His arm, omnipotence to thwart, —
    In mad rebellion all his days.

O Sovereign Grace, thine aid impart!
    Let not my soul thus foolish be!
Thy kingdom come within my heart!
    Reign there to all eternity!

How dark the mystery of sin !
That man should choose to dwell in night,
Refuse to let his Saviour in,
And close his eyes against thy light !

Oh, wondrous mystery of love !
Jesus has banished death's dark night ;
He lifts our souls to soar above
And dwell with him in heavenly light !

TIME.

ALL time is past; the future hour
  Not yet begins to be;
The present, the mere line that parts
  Time from eternity.

Exhaustless stores of good and ill
  Hid in the future lie; .
But ours the choice, which part to seize
  As they come floating by.

And time's the record of the choice,
  To fill with joy or shame
The soul, when Jesus' word shall come
  The judgment to proclaim.

ANNIVERSARY HYMN.

GOD, from eternity changeless in being,
  Guiding all changes by thy sovereign will,
Boundless in power, and in wisdom unerring,
  Ages of history thy counsels fulfil.

Tempest and earthquake, our labors o'erturning,
  Ever thy servants, obey thy command ;
Nations and kingdoms in vain would resist thee :
  Thou art almighty, and none can withstand.

Thanks for the light in our darkness still shining ;
  Thanks for the Word which came down from
    above ;
Thanks that thy Spirit within us bears witness
  We are thy children, and heirs of thy love !

Thou wert the merciful God of our fathers ;
  Still on their sons let thy blessing descend ;
Age after age may their praise and thanksgiving
  Rise in full harmony, world without end !

PROVIDENCE.

My God, thou art the bounteous source
　Of every joy my heart has known;
My every hope of future bliss
　Is built on thee, on thee alone.

Thou givest, and thou tak'st away;
　Unchanging still in love thou art.
Let neither gift nor loss arouse
　Or pride or murmuring in my heart.

I would remember thou art God!
　All-good, all-wise, almighty, thou;
I bid my feeble ignorance
　Before thy wise decisions bow.

With patient, longing, earnest faith
　I wait to see the scenes unrolled;
Assured that each can but display
　Thy boundless grace, thy love untold.

THE STORM.

O God! these tumults of my heart
  Lie open to thy sight;
Send forth thy dove to calm the waves;
  Guide thou my course aright.

These wilful longings and desires
  Restrain within thy will;
Oh, let the voice of Jesus bid
  Their raging waves be still!

Teach thou my heart to know that since
  All being flows from thee,
No joy desired outside thy will
  A real good can be.

No more these shadows I'll pursue,
  Amid a stormy night;
O Morning Star of endless day,
  I turn to thee for light!

REDEEMING LOVE.

O LORD! the riches of thy grace
    As far transcend my sorest needs
As thy blue heaven's unbounded space
    Outspreads the circle of my deeds.

I sank beneath my weight of woe,
    Beneath the burden of my fears;
Thy grace bade every terror go,
    And changed to laughter all my tears.

Black was the night my sins had made;
    Sore anguish racked my troubled breast;
Thy grace dispelled the fearful shade,
    And bathed my soul in heavenly rest.

How infinite my debt, O Lord!
    Yet I beheld in Jesus' face,
I heard in his life-giving word,
    The pledge of thy forgiving grace.

My trust is still thy boundless love ;
  My strength is thine almighty arm ;
Nor time nor death my faith shall move ;
  Not hell itself thy child can harm.

ΠΑΡΟΥΣΙΑ.

WHEN the risen Lord appears,
  Meeting with the faithful ten,
Swift he scatters doubts and fears,
  Kindling hope and faith again, —

Hope that grows no longer dim,
  Faith that henceforth never faints;
Fixing still their hearts on him,
  Strength and life of all his saints.

Lo! his presence with us here
  In all patient, faithful hearts
Banishes our doubt and fear,
  Life eternal still imparts.

If we listen for his voice,
  We shall hear his " Peace to you!
Ye shall in my joy rejoice,
  If with me God's work ye do."

ALL SAINTS.

ALL the saints, with one accord,
  Their " Non nobis " ever raise :
" Faith and strength are from the Lord ;
  Give to Christ alone the praise."

Those who won a martyr's fame,
  Heroes crowned, and victors, say
From the Lord their triumph came,
  At his feet their trophies lay.

These, with millions who have borne,
  Silent, their appointed load,
Crowned but with the piercing thorn,
  Have their honor still with God.

They " Non nobis " on their knees
  Raise to Christ alone ; but he :
" Father, I have given these
  Glory as thou gavest me."

"IN HIM WE LIVE."

WHAT depths profound, what topless height,
  What wondrous power in ceaseless flow,
What fulness of o'erpowering light,
  Thy works, my God, each moment show!

Thy word from everlasting stands;
  Upholding still the countless host,
'Twixt boundless seas and boundless lands,
  On Time's illimitable coast.

That word, incarnate in thy Son,
  O'er every nation pours its light;
The holy Church from him alone
  Draws wisdom, holiness, and might.

Through him still let thy Spirit send
  Eternal life, a constant tide;
Hope, faith, and love in us to blend,
  And with us ever to abide.

"OF HIM ARE ALL THINGS."

ETERNAL God! whose sovereign word
  The astonished depths of chaos heard,
When countless stars to being sprang,
  And praise to their Creator sang,

Thy Word incarnate from the night
  Of heathen darkness called out light,
And taught thy holy Church to sing
  The dazzling glories of her King.

Still give, O Lord, thy Word success;
  Renew its power to save and bless!
Too long the lingering shadows stay,
  And moral darkness clouds our day.

That light which once the Syrian sun
  In noonday brilliance far outshone
Again can lead new Pauls to be
  Ambassadors for Christ and thee.

EMANCIPATION.

IN THE NAME OF THE AFRICO-AMERICANS.

WE groped in murky night,
Beneath our burden bent,
When, like a flash of heavenly light,
The Lord deliverance sent.

The startled nations saw,
Amid a heavy cloud,
His sword the awful angel draw,
While thunders pealed aloud.

" Let ye God's people go ! "
The threatening voices cried ;
" The avenging blow must fall, and who
Its coming may abide ? "

That glittering sword and strong,
Swayed by that mighty hand,
Fierce smote the trebled cords of wrong,
And severed every strand.

Oh, praise the righteous Lord!
Give thanks unto his name!
'T was through his Spirit and his Word
That our deliverance came.

Accept, O Lord, our praise;
Make us more truly free,
And help us consecrate our days
In righteousness to thee.

VESPERS.

WHEN the bell for evening prayer
Floats upon the tranquil air,
My feet shall seek the holy shrine
Where the saints their voices join ;
And already swells the song, —
　　Eleison, Kyrie, soson, eleison.
Lo ! their prayer, to heaven ascending,
　　Lifts my soul with theirs.

Thus the bell for evening prayer,
Floating on the hallowed air,
Still leads my heart to find its rest
Pillowed on his sacred breast,
Who endured the cross for me.
　　Eleison, Kyrie, soson, eleison ;
And his grace, from heaven descending,
　　Fills my soul with peace.

A PRAYER.

1863.

HEAR our prayer, Lord God of the holy martyrs !
Give us strength, hope, courage, to bear the burden
Laid by thine all-holy appointment on us, —
    Burden of sorrow.

Still our tears flow fast for our falling kindred,
Slain by wounds, slain too in the fearful prisons, —
Starved till life, grown weak in the awful struggle,
    Gives up the contest;

Flow for those who, touched with a sharper sorrow,
Weep for sons laid low, or for husbands fallen ;
Flow for love's hopes quenched ere the bridal
    morning
    Shone on the maiden.

Hear our prayer, Lord, fountain of every virtue ;
Make our hearts beat strong with a holy purpose ;
Let our path grow clear as we press with ardor
    Forward to serve thee.

Let us not, through fear of a longer struggle,
Yield to those whose pride would destroy the nation,
So that they may lord it the more securely
    Over their bondmen.

Let us each, still guided in all our action
By the hand which thou hast outstretched to save us,
Dare to do what duty may lie before us,
    Pleasant or painful.

Work through us thine own ever-righteous purpose ;
Teach our hearts that strength and that hope and
      courage
Lie in thee alone, and in yielding gladly
    All to thy guidance.

SIC ITUR.

WISDOM leaves the haughty mind
　To its pride and self-conceit;
But the humble, docile soul
　Seeking her she comes to meet.

They who know of Nature most
　Know how slight their knowledge is,
Consecrating unto her
　All their holiest energies.

" Ever learning while you live,"
　Is the motto of the wise, —
Looking still on Nature's book
　With admiring, patient eyes.

'T is a book whose every page
　Shines with clear and holy light.
Pride is blind; while love alone
　Reads the glorious word aright.

OPENING A HOSPITAL.

ALMIGHTY God! we own thy power,
　Thy wisdom and thy love we see,
Nor strain our thought to sound the depths
　Which thou hast hid in mystery.

Why thou dost suffer sin to reign,
　Or death to fill the world with woe,
Or pain to overthrow the mind,
　Thou hast not given man to know.

But as from chaos, at thy word,
　Leaped forth the light's refulgent beam,
So out of sin and pain and death
　Thou causest charity to stream.

When thy dear Son sent forth his twelve
　To preach the living word from heaven,
" Go, heal the sick," he said, " and give
　As God to you has freely given."

To us thou givest freely; we·
  Would heal the sick, would comfort pain,
And bring the weak, o'erburdened one
  To strength and light and life again.

Accept, O God, this day, these walls
  As offerings made through Christ to thee;
At his command we consecrate
  This house to serve humanity.

AD ANIMAM.

Whither, mid pathless seas,
And tossed by restless billows to and fro,
Thy course dependent on the shifting breeze, —
      Say, whither dost thou go?

Let not, my soul, thy helm
Be held by earthly passions' fitful sway,
Lest sudden tempests should thy bark o'erwhelm,
      And night eclipse thy day.

Drift not alone, afar!
Thy guide to heaven be God's incarnate Word;
He leads the way, — that bright and morning Star,
      Thy Saviour, Christ the Lord.

A WINTER SKETCH.

I DID not know the child, but thought
 His years, perhaps, were ten;
Ah! seldom shall these eyes behold
 So sweet a sight again!

The little girl upon his sled
 Might not be more than eight;
She was as proud to see his strength
 As he to feel her weight.

I watched his little manly ways,
 His vigorous step but slow,
And saw her tucking close her skirts
 To keep them from the snow.

A glowing stream of golden hair
 Flowed freely down her back;
He fixed his eye alone to choose
 The smoothest, safest track.

Now which, I ask, enjoyed the most, —
The girl, the boy, or I?
Did she the ride, the honor he,
Or I their going by?

1843-1883.

WE met in Academus' grove;
  The flowers were wet with early dew,
The affluent morning from her stores
  Shed o'er each scene a roseate hue.

The birds poured out their sweetest notes,
  The air was tremulous with song;
Our hearts responded to their strains,
  And gladly would the hour prolong.

Yet in the horizon rose the peaks
  Of science, art, and noble fame;
With high ambition forth we went,
  With firm resolve and worthy aim.

The day wore on; our paths diverged;
  Then heat and storm and dangers rose.
Some conquered; but alas! some fell, —
  Yet with their faces toward their foes.

No paths divergent turned our hearts,
  Nor stormy winter ever chilled
The warmth of friendship which at first
  With sacred fire our hearts had filled.

Again we meet ; the westering sun
  Declares the noonday past for all :
Soon shall the deepening shades of night
  Around our every pathway fall.

Before they fall, may evening skies,
  Aglow with golden splendor bright,
Be pledge of an immortal day,
  Refulgent with eternal light.

FANCY'S MICROPHONE.

A new Meeting-House was built in Walpole, N. H., in 1789, and moved in 1826 to the centre of the village. It was used until 1842 both as a meeting-house and as a town-hall ; after that, as a town-hall only. Father Taylor preached in it once, on a week-day evening, in 1844. In 1886 it was remodelled, and reopened Feb. 1, 1887 ; and the following impromptu was read on that occasion.

'T IS sixty years since ! Thus the wizard wrote
   Whose magic pen entranced the human race.
'T is sixty years since, faithful history writes, —
   That these firm timbers found this resting-place.

Ah ! could some magic touch call back the sounds
   Which first and last have made their fibres thrill,
With what a rapt attention we should hear,
   What mingled feelings would our bosoms fill !

Come, Fancy's microphone, assist our sense ;
   No old Cremona, in a master's hand,
Waits more obedient to pour forth its tones
   Than now these timbers wait for thy command.

Hark ! first a woodland melody begins,
  Of branches rustling in a summer breeze ;
While squirrels chatter, and the insects chirp,
  And birds are singing in the leafy trees.

And next the woodman, with remorseless axe,
  Cuts short this harmony of grateful sound ;
Before his sturdier blows the sturdy oaks
  Soon yield, and crashing fall upon the ground.

Then, what a medley of confusing noise, —
  Of axe and saw ; of mallet, chisel, plane ;
Of nails that sink beneath the hammer's blow,
  Till in new form the timbers stand again !

Now hearken to the sound of holy psalm,
  Of fervent prayer, of argument, and plea
Made in the Master's name, that men in chains
  Of sin should look to him to set them free.

Richly among those pleas re-echoes one
  Made when this house to other use was turned.
Hark ! what a solemn hush came o'er the throng ;
  Within their hearts what solemn fervor burned !

"Praise ye the Lord," the theme the preacher chose:
"Praise him by loving man whom he has made."
With wondrous power upon that theme he spoke;
At his own will his hearers' hearts he swayed.

Laughter and tears alternate filled the hall;
With shame and high resolve each bosom swelled:
The coldest, sternest hearts were melted there;
The giddiest mind to close attention held.

Never again such eloquence as that
The fibres of this oaken frame may thrill;
Nor such a mingled tide of holy thought
And holy feeling every bosom fill.

But oft hereafter, as in decades past,
May words of kindness, words of friendly cheer,
Words of wise counsel, words of love and truth,
Be heard within these walls for many a year.

St. Louis, Mo., Feb. 5, 1887.

TRANSLATIONS AND IMITATIONS.

CUPID.

'T WAS about the hour of midnight,
When the Bear his course was changing,
'Neath the guidance of Boötes,
And the tribes of weary mortals,
By their labors tired, were sleeping,
When, before my cottage standing,
Little Cupid shook the door-latch ;
" Who is that," I cried, " there knocking,
And my pleasant dream has scattered ? "

Then he answered, " Open quickly !
I 'm a little boy, — don't fear me ;
But I 'm wet with dew, and wander,
Having lost my way, by starlight."

Then his story roused my pity ;
So my lamp I quickly lighted,

And I opened. There an urchin
I beheld, with bow and quiver,
And with wings upon his shoulders.
So I set him by the hearthstone,
While I rubbed his hands to warm them,
And brushed the chilling dewdrops
From his pretty curling ringlets.
But no sooner was he thawing
Than he cried, " I must examine
If this bow — I mean the bowstring —
Has been injured by the dampness."

Then he drew the bow and shot me,
Like a gadfly, in the liver ;
And in tones of exultation,
" Give me joy," he cried, " O stranger !
For my bow is good as ever ;
But your heart will give you trouble."

ANACREONTIC.

I WISHED to speak of Cadmos,
  The Atridæ I would sing ;
But still my harp resounded
  Of love, in every string.
I changed the strings for others,
  And tuned anew each wire ;
But when I sang Alcides,
  Of love still sang the lyre.
Farewell, then, every hero ;
  Ye sages, all farewell !
Of Loves and Cupids only
  My lyre will ever tell.

BEAUTY.

To oxen horns, to horses
Their hoofs, had Nature given;
To timid hares their fleetness,
And fearful teeth to lions;
To fish, the power of swimming;
To birds, the power of flying;
To man, of understanding.
What, then, was left for woman?
What could she give her? — Beauty,
Above all other weapons,
Offensive or defensive.
She conquers even iron,
Or fire, whom beauty aideth.

FROM SAPPHO.

BLEST as a god he seems to me —
More highly blest, could that thing be —
Who, seated near, may list to thee
    And see thy smile so sweet.
But yet that smile my senses stole;
And when I saw thee, love, my soul
O'er all my members lost control.
    My pulse refused to beat;
My tongue in vain to speak essayed;
Soft in my ears low murmurs played;
Dim grew my swimming eyes, afraid
    Again that glance to meet.

SAPPHO'S PRAYER.

IMMORTAL Venus! on mosaic throne,
Thou child of crafty Jove, I call on thee!
Oh, not with sorrow nor with care subdue,
    Goddess, my spirit.

But hither come, if ever heretofore,
My prayer receiving with attentive ear,
Thou heardst, and from the house of Father Jove
    Hither didst hasten;

Thy golden chariot driving, drawn by birds,
So swift and beauteous, o'er the dark-brown earth,
Their wings all fluttering in the lofty heaven,
    Through the mid-ether.

They quickly came; and thou, O blessed one,
With smiles upon thine ever-living face,
Asked what I suffered, why I called on thee,
    Seeking thy presence,

And what might be the dearest wish within
My raging heart: "For whom shall I prepare
The snares of blinding love? or who treats thee,
    Sappho, unjustly?

"For if he flies, he quickly shall pursue;
If gifts he takes not, he shall bring them thee;
If now he curses, he shall quickly kiss
    Thee, though thou wish not."

Again come to me now, and set me free
From grievous cares; all that my heart desires
To do, do thou; thyself become for me
    Helper and ally!

14

EIGENTHUM.

FROM GOETHE.

I KNOW that nothing is mine own
Except the quiet thoughts alone
   Which in my soul arise, —
These, and each happy passing hour
Which on me some benignant power
   Sheds from the changing skies.

HOFFNUNG.

FROM GOETHE.

MAY each day's labor of my hand,
By fortune favored, finished stand;
   Nor let me faint, nor fear.
This wish shall be no idle dream;
For on these trees, though bare they seem,
   Shall leaves and fruit appear.

GANYMEDE.

FROM GOETHE.

How in the morning brightness
Thou around me glowest,
Spring, my beloved !
With thousand-fold endearments
On my heart impressing
Thine eternal warmth,
Holy passion,
Infinite beauty.
Oh, that I might clasp thee
  In these arms !

Ah, on thy bosom
I lie, I languish ;
And thy grass, thy flowers,
Are impressed upon my heart.
Thou coolest the burning
Thirst of my bosom,

Lovely morning wind !
Therein the nightingale calls
Fondly to me from the mist vale.
I come, I come !
Whither, ah ! whither ?
Upward, upward is the struggle.
The clouds are floating
Downward, the clouds
Bow themselves to the longing love.
Me !   I !
To your caresses,
Upwards,
All-surrounding embrace !
Upwards to thy bosom,
All-loving Father !

ABSCHIED.

FROM GOETHE.

LET my eyes the farewell utter
  Which my lips in vain essay;
Hard, too hard, for me to bear it,
  Though a man until to-day!

Sad to me, at such an hour,
  Sweetest pledge of love would be,
Of thy hand how slight the pressure!
  Cold the kiss thou givest me!

Once a kiss, though slyly stolen,
  Filled my heart with rapture sweet,
Pleasant as the violet's odor,
  Which in early March we meet.

But no violet now I gather,
  Roses pluck no more for thee;
Spring they call it, dearest maiden,
  But 't is sombre fall for me.

DAS VEILCHEN.

FROM GOETHE.

A VIOLET in the meadow green
Bowed down its head with modest mien ;
    It was a charming flower.
There came a lovely maiden there ;
With happy heart and joyous air
    She came, she came,
Blithe singing in the meadow fair.

"Ah !" thought the violet, "could I be
The fairest of all flowers to see !
    If 't were but half an hour,
Till, charming my beloved's eye,
She plucked me, on her breast to lie,
    And, withering there,
In ecstasy of bliss to die !"

Then nearer came the maiden fair,
Nor saw the violet blooming there,
    But careless crushed the flower.

It sank, and, dying, sweetly said,
"No pain to die beneath her tread;
    No pain to die
Through her, and at her feet lie dead."

FROM THEODORE STORM.

How sweet, at leisure, by the loved one's side
To rest upon the mountain's sunlit head,
With town and country underneath you spread,
    To gaze at will o'er all the landscape wide!

Delicious quiet, — silently to stand
And breathe the earliest odors of the Spring,
While zephyrs still their invitations bring
    To sail with them o'er all the enchanted land!

Then, as you turn from all this wondrous sight,
Her yet more wondrous eyes give new delight.

MORNING HYMN.

FROM SCHILLER'S " MACBETH."

THE shades of night have passed away, .
The lark salutes the rising day,
The sunrise is already nigh, —
Its splendors gleam athwart the sky;
They gild alike the palace hall
And lowly cotter's mud-built wall:
The secrets which in darkness lay
Stand now revealed in open day.

Oh, praise and thank the Lord alway !
He watches o'er us night and day.
A host of angels still he sends,
And faithfully the house defends.
While many close their eyes, by night,
In death, nor see the morning light,
Let those rejoice whose opening eyes,
Refreshed, behold the sun arise.

SCHILLER'S REMONSTRANCE.

TALK not to me, Astronomers, always of stars and
of motion !
Worlds had never been made simply for science to
count.
Grand is heaven's host, doubtless; in space there
is nothing sublimer ;
But, good friends, the sublime was n't embodied
in space.

THE ASTRONOMER'S REPLY.

SPACE, time, spirit, these three, are revealed to
the mind of the finite ;
Each in that order appears, flooding the soul with
its light.
Never arises the third — the godlike effulgénce of
spirit —
Till through the stars stand revealed traces of
infinite thought.

THE CONCERT OF THE SPHERES.

ABRIDGED FROM PFEFFEL.

A YOUTH, in Plato, chanced to see
Something about the harmony
Of heavenly spheres. "I 'll hear," quoth he,
"This music." So great Jove he prays
To let him hear. "Young fool!" Jove says,
"The godlike concert of the spheres
Was never made for mortal ears."
But still he begged, till Jove one day
Resolved to let him have his way.
He nods his head; the youngster found
He heard, — but what? A crash of sound,
To which a thousand Orcan tongues
Which horror and destruction rung,
And all the thunders, by the hand
Of Jove sent over every land,
Were like the humming of a bee.
"O Jove!" all stiff and pale, cried he;

" Is that the heavenly harmony?
So roars the yawning gulf of hell!
Oh, make me deaf, or break the spell!"
Then answered Jove from out the clouds:
" Weak child of earth, men are not gods;
You hear a frightful noise, while I
Hear heaven's all-perfect harmony."

FROM CHAMISSO.

THEY vex me much, these many trials how
  To make the earth turn back from east to west.
  'T would grieve me less did foolish men think best
To help her turn from west to east, as now.

Fool, to be vexed! As in the book of fate
  The word is written, shall the ages flow;
  The earth shall steadfast in her courses go.
Thy wrath is vain ; it falls on thine own pate.

I know full well my judgment they despise.
  I cannot change them ; let their folly run !
Be still, my heart! thine anger is not wise.
Yet, when I hear them, great in their own eyes,
  Each other praise, "How bravely we get on!"
Then, hang them all! my anger still will rise.

CHAMISSO TO HIS WIFE.

WHETHER I love thee?   How that question ask?
   Or how could any words that doubt remove?
   My life alone to thee my love can prove,
And words are all unequal to the task.

Whether my love will last?   I pity her
   To whom an oath could such assurance give.
   Oaths are but oaths, — mere words; like leaves,
      they live
While Summer's breath may vital power confer.

"How canst thou, naughty man, thus try my heart?
   What could I mean, but that I wished to hear
Thy lips declare my joy!   Thou cross, sweet love!"
Thou holiest, purest, from the choirs above,
   Yet mine!   My pet, my wife, my strength, my
      cheer,
My being's all, my life, my love, thou art!

FROM THEREMIN.

My childhood's days had quickly passed away,
   And also fled full soon the times of youth,
   Yet thee, O Lord, I had not known; in truth,
'T was utter blindness held me in its sway.

My riper years with better days were filled;
   Then first appeared to me thy glorious light:
   'T was thou didst heal my wounds, restore my
      sight;
My heart's unconscious longings thou hast stilled.

And as my age increased, thy power dispersed
   All darkness; for thou mad'st my strength abound
To soar on eagle's wings above this earth.
Thus in my life have all things been reversed:
   Young, I was old; in age my youth I found;
Soon shall I find in death immortal birth!

SONGS BY HEINE.

I.

MID the wondrous beauty of May,
  When every bud is swelling,
The fathomless tides of love
  Within my heart are welling.

Mid the wondrous beauty of May,
  When every bird is singing,
The tortures of longing and love
  From me this confession are wringing.

II.

FROM my falling tear-drops
  Blooming flowers arise;
Nightingales are singing
  In my tender sighs.

Wilt thou love me, maiden,
  The flowers to thee I'll bring;
Nightly 'neath thy window
  Those nightingales shall sing.

III.

THE rose and the lily, the dove and the sun, —
  I once loved them all, and was happy in loving.
I love them no more; I now love but one, —
  The dear one, the fair one, the pure one, worth
    loving;
She herself is the fountain whence all love doth run;
She 's the rose and the lily, the dove and the sun.

IV.

WHEN I look into thine eyes,
Half my pain and sorrow flies;
But kisses on thy mouth impart
Perfect soundness to my heart.

Leaning on thy breast, I feel
Heavenly pulses o'er me steal;
Yet when thou own'st thou lovest me,
I must weep, weep bitterly.

V.

THY face, so beautiful and dear,
I saw last night in dreams appear;
It beamed with soft and holy light,
And yet so pale, so deadly white.

Thy lips alone retain their glow,
And Death shall kiss them white as snow, —
Shall quench for aye the heavenly light
With which thine angel eyes are bright.

15

FROM HEINE.

Ah! did the little flowerets know
  The deep wounds of my heart,
Their tears would quick begin to flow
  To heal the bitter smart.

If to the nightingales 't was known
  How faint with grief am I,
Their cheering, sympathetic tone
  Would ring through all the sky.

And did the golden stars above
  My heart's deep sorrow know,
They'd whisper from the heavens their love,
  And thus console my woe.

But these the secret have not found;
  One only knows my pain :
'T is she that gave the aching wound,
  And tore my heart in twain.

A MYSTERY.

WHY should my heart, on seeing her,
　Thus thrill with dreamy bliss?
These arms can ne'er enfold her,
　These lips can never kiss.

From her dear face the sunshine,
　Soft falling on my heart,
Perfects its magic vintage
　With quick, unconscious art.

Oh, wine of love, enchanting
　To every wish and thought!
Beside thy heavenly rapture
　All other bliss is naught.

These arms may ne'er enfold her,
　These lips can never kiss;
Still shall my heart, on seeing her,
　Be thrilled with dreamy bliss.

SONG.

THE sun is gone; the blushing west
Now takes him to her glowing breast,
While from the east the violet night
Sweeps on with swift and noiseless flight.

But cold and dark would be the sun
Beside my love, belovèd one!
Nor are the fixèd stars of night
So changeless as the troth I plight.

FROM THE GREEK ANTHOLOGY.

—◆—

EPITAPHS.

HERE rests, in sacred sleep, Acanthios the just :
Say not the good can die, though dust return to
    dust.

A MORNING star in loveliness wert thou, dear
    child ;
Thy memory, an evening star, now sheds its radiance
    mild.

I DIED, and wait for thee.   So shalt thou die, and
    wait
In that one grave where all are brought by fate.

Now, chance and hope, farewell !   I 've reached
    the port :
No more I fear ; make who survive, your sport.

THIS man was a beggar; but now that he 's dead,
No lower than Xerxes he layeth his head.

HERE 's a crusty old fool who ne'er took a wife;
Would his father had lived, too, a bachelor's life!

———◆———

MISCELLANEOUS.

To be valiant, not wise, is surely an evil;
Without wisdom, boldness but leads to the Devil.

GNAW me down (said the vine), Master Goat, to
  the root;
Long after you 're dead I will grow and bear fruit.

WHAT! Medon's picture? There 's no likeness
  in it;
He never ceases babbling for a minute.

" NICYLLA dyes her hair," some may have thought;
But I suspect 't was black when first 't was bought.

A MISER cried out, when he saw a poor mouse,
"Pray, what are you doing, you scamp, in my
  house?"
"Fear nothing, dear sir," said the mouse, with a
  smile;
"I came not for board, but for lodgings awhile."

WHEN I chance to see Iphicus, think it no wonder
My tongue will in sympathy stumble and blunder.

OLD Grip chanced to dream that he once gave
  a dinner;
The dream was so horrid it waked the old sinner.

TEN thousand times I've sworn no more to write,
And by my satire gain from fools their spite;
But, seeing Cleon's shallow face, again,
Spite of my vows, I itch to use my pen.

NEW complexion, new hair, and new teeth she
  can buy;
What would not she give, could she get a new
  eye?

NOTES.

THE MARSH, p. 18. — Some critics, noticing certain of my verses as they have appeared in magazines, have spoken of them as attempts to write English verse by the Latin rules of quantity. This is a total misunderstanding. The verses are to be read with simply the English accent. The choriambics in this volume (in "The Marsh," "The Mile Run," "Bloodroot," etc.) have nothing more to do with Latin quantity than the iambics (as in "Symplocarpus") have. The only attempts to write English by Latin rules, which I remember, are two of Tennyson's, — "O you chorus of indolent reviewers," and "O mighty-mouthed inventor of harmonies."

MANDRAKE, p. 25. — Not the real mandrake, but the American mandrake, or May-apple, — *Podophyllum.*

TO A PHYSALIA, p. 66. — The Physalia, or Portuguese Man-of-war, is also called the Sea-Nettle, from its extraordinary power of nettling or stinging, in which it far exceeds other Acalephs. As it is usually seen floating on tropical seas, sustained by a brilliantly colored balloon, it consists of a Siamese brotherhood of offspring surrounding a parent, to which, also, they are united by the closest organic ties, each member of the group having its own functions. Some manage the balloon; others send down long lassos after prey; a few eat and digest for the whole; still others are wholly occupied in producing and in fertilizing eggs, from which new parents may arise.

TRANSLATIONS AND IMITATIONS. — The word "Imitations," in this title, refers to "A Mystery" (p. 227) and "Song" (p. 228), in which the style of thought and expression in other writers was aimed at, without reference to particular poems. The remainder are properly translations, — attempts to reproduce the thought, the spirit, and in most cases even the rhythm, of the original poems, rather than to create English poems in imitation of them.

FROM CHAMISSO, p. 221.— Chamisso, so well known as a lyric poet, was also a professional botanist; and in a letter to De la Foye, January, 1824, laments that men were more eager to write out their theories of evolution and the like than to observe, and then appends this sonnet. Agassiz (Contributions to the Natural History of the United States, vol. i. p. 53), by referring Darwinists to the more playful lines sent to the same correspondent two years earlier, beginning, —

" 'S war Einer, dem 's zu Herzen ging,"

appears to think that they refer to the same theme. They may be thus rendered : —

> There was a man whose heart it wrung
> Because his queue behind him hung;
>   He otherwise would have it.
>
> He thinks, " How shall it be begun ?
> I 'll turn me round, and then 't is done."
>   The queue, it hangs behind him.
>
> He quickly turns himself around;
> It did no good, for still he found
>   The queue, it hangs behind him.
>
> He turns to th' left, he turns to th' right;
> Nor worse nor better is his plight, —
>   The queue, it hangs behind him.
>
> He whirls like any humming-top,
> But all in vain; for, go or stop,
>   The queue, it hangs behind him.
>
> And lo! he 's spinning still so fast,
> And thinks 't will come in front at last;
>   The queue, it hangs behind him.

The temptation to append here a still earlier piece of this poet's playfulness is irresistible. It will be remembered that his famous story of "Peter Schlemihl" had made Schlemihl a common noun in Germany, signifying an idle, worthless fellow.

Chamisso was botanist in the first scientific expedition, led by Kotzebue (son of the dramatist), in the Pacific Ocean, and complains that the name "Chamissonis," attached by his scientific friends to plants, insects, or islands, did not increase his income : —

Who gave that Carabus to me,
Yet left it by the Alaskan sea?
  'T was Dr. Eschscholtz' gift, so nice ;
  'T is he distributes bugs and lice.
    He gave that Carabus to me,
    Yet left it by the Alaskan Sea.

Who gave me, out of rich Peru,
As cheap a weed as ever grew?
  That youngster Kunth, without a qualm,
  Gave Achyranthes, — not a palm.
    He gave me, out of rich Peru,
    As cheap a weed as ever grew.

Who gave me, mid the polar seas,
A nest of rocks where brandy 'd freeze?
  'T was Kotzebue, who can divide
  At his own will the land and tide,
    Yet gave me, mid the polar seas,
    A nest of rocks where brandy 'd freeze.

A nest of rocks is no soft bed,
And Achyranthes is not bread ;
  Alaskan bugs no gold disburse ;
  My heart is heavy, not my purse.
    A nest of rocks is no soft bed,
    And Achyranthes is not bread.

Ah ! would some chap would give to me,
Or churl or emperor his degree,
  Full honors payable in gold,
  In monthly portions duly told !
    Ah, that would be the chap for me,
    Or churl or emperor his degree !

But no man, no man, thinks of that:
A Schlemihl 's always a poor rat ;
  And I, the father of the race,
  Must with their poverty keep pace.
    Yet no man, no man, thinks of that :
    A Schlemihl 's always a poor rat.

THE END.

www.ingramcontent.com/pod-product-compliance
Lightning Source LLC
Chambersburg PA
CBHW020112030726

47498CB00006B/2070